THE LION'S GATE

On holiday with her wayward sister Allison at a lakeside town, Peggy Conners is perplexed when Allison packs her bags and vanishes overnight, without explanation. Believing her sister to be in great danger, Peggy eventually traces and confronts her, now living on an island at the Lions family mansion. But then Allison asserts that her name is actually Melissa Lions — and that she has never seen Peggy before in her life!

V. J. BANIS

THE LION'S GATE

Complete and Unabridged

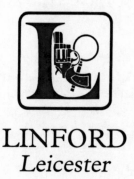

LINFORD
Leicester

First published in Great Britain

First Linford Edition
published 2016

A catalogue record for this book is available
from the British Library.

ISBN 978–1–4448–2698–2

Published by
F. A. Thorpe (Publishing)
Anstey, Leicestershire

Set by Words & Graphics Ltd.
Anstey, Leicestershire
Printed and bound in Great Britain by
T. J. International Ltd., Padstow, Cornwall

This book is printed on acid-free paper

1

Allison had always been a problem, from the first day when, as a girl of five, she'd wandered onto the front steps of the Connerses' summer cottage at Hunter's Point. No one knew anything about her . . . where she came from, who her family was, how she happened to show up there. Allison herself could remember nothing. Not then, not ever.

Of course, the Connerses had taken her in, and they had been allowed to keep her while the authorities tried, without success, to trace her family. In time, the Connerses had unofficially adopted the little girl and loved her like their own.

That wasn't always easy. From the beginning she had been difficult, a moody, temperamental child who grew into a defiant, brooding young woman. The Connerses 'made allowances'.

Perhaps more than anyone else, Peggy Conners made allowances. From the first day she adopted Allison as her younger sister, although there was only two years' difference in their ages. Peggy had always been grown-up beyond her years, however. 'A born mother,' Mrs. Conners had long said of her only child. And Peggy, the born mother, had quickly taken under her wing the moody, withdrawn little sister who had appeared so mysteriously as though in answer to Peggy's secret, silent prayer.

'Please, God, bring me a little sister to play with,' she had prayed, and just like that, Allison appeared at the door.

'There's no clue who she belongs to,' the police had said, but Peggy knew, she knew who Allison belonged to. Allison belonged to her.

Of course, she spoiled her.

'Just as you're spoiling her now.' Mrs. Conners made no secret of her disapproval of Peggy's plan.

'I don't see how you can say that. You told her she couldn't have a trip to Europe, which was what she wanted. All I'm doing is suggesting we spend the summer at the lake instead. You can't

2

really say she's being spoiled by being given a summer at Hunter's Point in lieu of a summer in Venice or Cannes, or wherever she had her heart set on.'

Peggy downed a last swallow of coffee and came to kiss her mother's cheek. She knew better than to take all this grumbling seriously. For all her stern conversation, Mrs. Conners — Maureen to her friends — was a soft-hearted, deeply loving person who, if she hadn't been so sorely tried over the last few years, and if Allison had persisted, probably would have given in on the European trip.

Peggy actually agreed with her mother. Considering Allison's school record, giving her a trip to Europe would have been an extreme indulgence.

'Summer trips are given as a reward,' Maureen Conners said argumentatively, although they both knew the argument was over. 'I just can't see rewarding Allison for getting expelled from school. After all, the reason we sent her there — and a private school is expensive, I don't need to remind you — is because she couldn't get along in a public school. And now this, kicked out! If you ask me, she needs to spend a summer right here in Columbus, Ohio, without privileges . . . '

'Mother, darling, you could no more 'ground' a girl of nineteen today than you could . . . '

'Than I could talk you out of your plans. And today at nineteen she's not a girl, she's a young woman.' Mrs. Conners sighed. 'Very well, do as you think best, but remember, whatever the outcome, this is your idea. Your father seems ready to wash his hands of Allison altogether and I'm not sure I'd be entirely at odds with that. We've done a great deal for her, you can't deny that, and I can't say she has ever shown the slightest evidence of gratitude.'

Peggy had heard all this before and had neither need nor desire to hear it again. She set her cup on the kitchen counter, grabbed her purse, and said, 'Bye,' in the middle of her mother's monologue.

She paused in the hall just long enough to run a comb through her long, dark hair, and she was out of the apartment.

She clambered into her battered Jaguar roadster and in a few minutes she was cutting in and out of the afternoon traffic, making for the airport.

She was ever aware of the admiring glances she got from men in passing cars. Of course it pleased her. 'Vanity, thy name is Peggy,' she teased herself, without taking any of it very seriously.

She looked forward to her reunion with Allison with mixed feelings. It would be nice to see Allison again. In many ways, they had been closer than real sisters might have been. On the other hand, she had no doubt Allison would be in a foul mood, having been refused the summer trip she had wanted. And when Allison was in a foul mood . . .

Peggy sighed. She hated having to deal with problems and, generally speaking, if there were a way to avoid trouble, she would find it. With Allison, however, that was sometimes just impossible to do.

She was surprised, when she saw Allison at the airport, how Allison had grown up over the last year. Not in size — it would be many years before Allison's slim, petite figure changed much — but the shy, awkward waif had given way to an attractive, determined young woman who strode purposefully toward the gate where Peggy waited. Peggy's usual pace, leisurely and graceful, was no match for Allison's swift progress along the corridor.

'It's good to see you,' Peggy said, hurrying to keep up.

'I'm surprised anyone even came for me. I thought I'd been disinherited.' Allison's mouth was set in a petulant expression. She tossed her head, sending her blonde hair shimmering.

'Oh, Allison, how can you say that? I've even been making plans for the summer, for just the two of us. I thought we'd leave right away for the lake — '

'The lake?' Allison stopped so abruptly that Peggy nearly went on by. 'Lake Erie?'

'Well, of course Lake Erie. We haven't been there in so long, we can be a couple of little kids . . . '

Allison began walking again, faster and more determined. 'I asked for a trip to Florence and Rome and I end up at

Hunter's Point? It's enough to make me want to turn right around and leave again.'

'Why don't you, then?' Peggy challenged her, feeling stung. 'No, seriously, if you find the prospect of a few weeks with me so distasteful, you certainly aren't under any obligation to do it. If you'd rather be somewhere else, then go wherever you want.'

'And what am I going to go on? Certainly not on the meager allowance the family doles out to me. I've barely been able to meet my school expenses out of that, let alone pay for a trip.'

Peggy half-opened her mouth to make the expected answer. In the past that sort of remark would have been quite enough to coax her to open her purse. She was always able to set aside a little out of her own allowance and she had never been stingy about sharing it with Allison, but this time her better judgment kicked in. Allison had been expelled from school, after all, and the European trip had been denied as a form of punishment. She couldn't satisfy Allison's every whim just to appease her anger. Instinctively, Peggy tightened her grip on her purse.

'That isn't fair. You know you get the same allowance that I get, and you always have.'

'Yes, but yours is supplemented. Every time you want something they always come through without a question. Of course, you are the *real* daughter, and I'm only an add-on.'

Peggy was tempted to reply sharply to that unfair remark, but they had reached the baggage area and were now surrounded by other passengers waiting for their luggage too.

'We'll talk about this when we get to the car,' she said firmly.

Allison's lower lip moved outward slightly but she kept her silence and began to scan the arriving bags, looking for hers — the expensive Vuitton set the family had given her when she went away, as Peggy was tempted to remind her.

By the time they were in the car, though, Peggy had regained her composure. 'Look,' she said as she drove out of the parking lot, 'this trip to the lake isn't mandatory for you, you know. Just because I'm going, you don't have to if you don't want to.'

'I thought the law was being laid down.' Allison was still petulant. Her long blonde hair whipped about her face in the wind. The admiring glances from passing males were definitely on the increase. Peggy, who knew she herself was attractive, had always felt somewhat awed by Allison's beauty.

'Not in the least. I just thought you'd enjoy being with me at the lake more than you would spending the next few weeks with the folks. But it's really up to you.'

There was a long silence while Allison digested that. Then, as Peggy had known she would, she sighed and said, 'I guess I'll go to the lake with you.'

'And I'll guess,' Peggy thought wryly but did not say, 'this is going to be a doozie of a vacation.'

She smiled as she whipped the Jag around a slow-moving delivery van in her path. Allison was simply angry now, and disappointed in not getting her way, but tomorrow night they would be at the lake, where they had first met and where they'd shared many girlhood adventures. Allison would work herself out of the sulks, and when Allison was in a good mood, she could be such fun. It would be just like old times.

At least, that was the way Peggy had planned it.

*   *   *

'The best-laid plans,' Peggy muttered to herself as she stepped onto the balcony of their little hotel room. Over the tops of the trees she could see the distant waters of the lake, crowded now with boats. The sun was sinking toward the horizon and most of the boats were headed in. Behind her, Peggy could hear the sound of the shower running. She was hungry and hoped Allison didn't linger too long in the bathroom.

The drive from Columbus to Hunter's Point took the better part of a day, and as the cottage had been closed up since the previous summer, they had decided it would be more practical to spend the night at Hunter's Point's old-fashioned hotel, and to tackle putting the cottage in order in the morning.

In truth, Peggy felt more like tackling her adopted sister. Allison's sulky mood had continued unabated throughout the entire drive. She had spoken only to answer Peggy's questions, and then in a petulant, often sarcastic manner. Peggy had begun to feel as if it were she who was being punished for Allison's misbehavior at school.

'Well, this was my own idea,' she reminded herself.

Behind her, she heard Allison, in the bedroom now, rummaging through her luggage. Peggy made herself smile and went back into the room. Allison was holding up a glamorous black dress that must have cost her an entire month's allowance.

'I got this with Paris in mind,' she said, tossing it carelessly onto the bed. 'I suppose it's a bit *de trop* for Hunter's Point.'

'Oh, I don't know, I suppose some of the farm women change from their coveralls before they come into town,'

11

Peggy said drily. She herself was wearing a flaring denim skirt with oversize pockets, and a simple checked blouse. She gave Allison an impetuous hug. 'Oh, come on, honey, this isn't the end of the world, you know. As long as we're here, why not enjoy ourselves?'

'I guess you're right.'

'I know I am. And I'm also starving, and as I recall, the food on the terrace is excellent . . . maybe not Paris or Rome, but by provincial standards very good. How about this print number? It's awfully pretty and should be cool.'

Although it was a small town, Hunter's Point was a popular resort area and consequently boasted a surprising number of good hotels and restaurants for a town its size. They had often, in the past, come here to the hotel to eat. In addition to the usual coffee shop and a rather over-decorated dining room, there was a really lovely terrace for summer dining, overhung with flower-entwined trellises and with a view of the lake.

Peggy had already called down to reserve a table and they were shown to it without delay. While they scanned the menus, Peggy ordered a bottle of wine. That brought her the first appreciative smile she had gotten so far from Allison.

'I was wondering if you'd get upset if I asked for a drink,' she said.

'Well, we *are* grown up now,' Peggy said. She sipped the wine and nodded approvingly. 'This is good. I don't know if you remember, it comes from around here, near Sandusky.'

Allison picked up the bottle to read the label. 'I suppose you chose this because of your astrological sign.'

'What do you mean?'

Allison pointed a finger at the label, dominated by two medieval-looking lions supporting a heraldic banner between them. 'Lions, the symbol of Leo,' she said. She read the print. ' "The House of Lions, Fine Wines". I guess I had forgotten that Ohio has a wine district.'

'Maybe we should take a tour of the winery,' Peggy suggested brightly.

Allison put the bottle down with a *thunk*. 'Somehow, I don't think it would measure up to Burgundy or one of the other French wine-growing districts.'

'It could be nice, anyway, if you'd let it be. But like everything else, if you approach it with your mind already made up that it's going to be a drag, it probably will be.'

'Shall we order?' Allison said, obviously wanting to get off the subject.

With that, Peggy gave her attention to the menu. They sat in cool silence waiting for their dinner to begin. Finally, too annoyed to care about making a further effort to cheer up Allison, Peggy pushed her chair back from the table.

'Now that the sun's gone it's getting chilly out here. I think I'll get myself a sweater. Can I bring you something?'

'No, I'm comfortable, thanks.'

On her way upstairs in the elevator, though, Peggy regretted having snapped at Allison. It took two to make a quarrel. After all, this was her vacation too, and if Allison chose to have a bad time there was no law that said she had to as well. She would go ahead with her own plans and Allison could join her or not as she wished.

When she returned to the terrace a few

minutes later, a lightweight sweater around her shoulders, she was surprised to discover Allison was no longer alone. An older, silver-haired woman had joined her at the table. It had been so many years since they had been to the lake that Peggy was surprised to see Allison still had any acquaintances here.

Allison and her visitor were talking animatedly, but as Peggy came across the terrace she saw Allison put a hand gently upon the older woman's hand, and both glance briefly in her direction. For a moment Peggy had the odd impression that Allison had warned her visitor of her approach, and their conversation had stopped.

'How silly,' she chided herself. As she walked up they began talking again.

'It's still cool in the evenings this time of year,' the stranger was saying. 'Wait a week or so and you'll wish it was like this again.'

She turned and smiled as Peggy joined them. 'Hello,' she said brightly.

'Oh, Peggy, this is Mrs. Denver. There were no tables available and I invited her to join us for a drink. You don't mind, do you?' Allison seemed to have recovered altogether from her bad mood.

'Not at all.' Peggy caught herself before she glanced around at the several empty tables nearby — probably, she told herself, all reserved. 'Are you staying here at the hotel too?'

'Yes, for a few days. Did you just arrive this evening?' The waitress set a martini in front of Mrs. Denver. Peggy wondered if her question were rhetorical. Surely, in the animated conversation she and Allison had been having, that fact must already have come out.

'Yes, but we'll only be at the hotel for tonight.'

'Oh, yes, you have a cottage on the lake. I forgot.' Mrs. Denver sipped her drink, her fingers leaving marks on the heavily-frosted glass.

She was, Peggy thought, a strange sort, dressed uniquely enough to seem almost eccentric. Although it was evening now, she wore a wide-brimmed hat with a veil that did not actually hide but tended to blur her features. She was big-boned and

16

probably tall, but she sat slumped in her chair, which made it difficult to tell.

'You're a Leo, aren't you?' Mrs. Denver asked unexpectedly.

'Why, yes,' Peggy said, momentarily surprised. 'Oh, but Allison must have told you that.'

'No need, it's obvious at a glance. The stateliness of bearing, the firm step, the Roman features, even the deliberation in the way you speak. No, my dear, I needed no one to tell me, I could see at a glance that you are the proud, royal sign.'

Despite herself, Peggy was flattered by the description. She had never really given any credence to the so-called science of astrology, but Mrs. Denver's observations certainly were intriguing. Had she really guessed the sign correctly, or had Allison told her? Allison wasn't letting the cat out of the bag if that were so.

The waitress arrived then with entrées for Peggy and Allison and the conversation dwindled. The food was good and Peggy was ravenous. The lake always seemed to perk up her appetite. Mrs.

Denver and Allison resumed talking about astrology. Mrs. Denver seemed quite knowledgeable on the subject. To Peggy's surprise, so did Allison. She'd never heard Allison discuss the topic before.

Peggy's chair was facing the door and as she glanced up she saw a man standing in the doorway staring at their table. He was huge, tall and thickly-built, with coarse features that seemed set in a permanent scowl. Something about him sent an involuntary shiver up Peggy's spine.

Mrs. Denver followed Peggy's glance toward the door. 'Oh, that's Waldo, my chauffeur. I'm afraid I must go.' She finished her cocktail and pushed her chair back, standing. 'It's been so pleasant chatting with you both. I hope we meet again.'

'I'm sure we shall,' Allison said warmly.

Peggy watched Mrs. Denver cross the terrace. She moved gracefully. Her walk, her dress, the authentic glimmer of her jewelry, all spoke of breeding, of class and wealth. Yet there was something about her that Peggy could not quite put her finger on, something not quite right. She watched Mrs. Denver and her brutish-looking chauffeur speak to each other for a moment.

Suddenly they both glanced back at the table. For the briefest of interludes, Peggy's eyes met those of the chauffeur. He looked away quickly, but even that brief contact had sent another shiver up Peggy's spine.

Mrs. Denver said something to him and walked away, and the big man followed.

'Now that's a strange pair,' Peggy said, sipping her coffee.

'Mrs. Denver? I thought she was very charming. Of course I didn't get a look at the chauffeur. What was his name, Walter?'

'Waldo. And lucky you. How about a stroll down to the landing?'

'Hmm? Oh, okay.'

It had seemed to Peggy while Mrs. Denver was at the table that Allison had recovered from her previous dark mood. But now, as they strolled along the darkening streets, Allison seemed to withdraw into herself.

She was thoughtful and uncommunicative, as if entirely wrapped up in some private consideration; and at length, despairing of any sort of companionship, Peggy announced that after all she was tired from the long drive, and perhaps they should just call it a day and get an early start the next morning at setting the cottage in order.

★   ★   ★

It did not take long to put the cottage in order. Dust covers had to be removed and the rooms needed a quick run-through with the vacuum cleaner. Peggy had called ahead to have the utilities turned on, and by midmorning things were relatively shipshape.

'That's about everything but the shopping,' Peggy announced. 'Let's get that out of the way before lunch, okay?'

Allison had apparently gotten over her sulks, but her private, withdrawn mood from the night before had continued. All morning long, while she had worked about the cottage, she had acted as if she were wrestling with some problem of her own.

'Why don't you go ahead?' she said

now. 'There are one or two things I'd like to do around here.'

'Look, there isn't something bothering you, is there? Something you want to talk about?'

Allison shook her head. 'No, not really. You go ahead, don't worry about me.'

For a moment Peggy was tempted to push the issue; then she thought better of it. 'Okay, see you in about an hour.'

She drove into the village, parking the car in the municipal lot, and walked around to do her errands. The phone still hadn't been connected, so she had to pay a visit to the phone company, and there were myriad things to be purchased at the hardware store — a new cord for the electric coffeemaker, the old one seeming to have taken flight over the winter; pins and needles and threads; a couple of odd cooking utensils to replace old ones that had been discarded or transported back to Columbus in the past — the busy-work of a summer cottage.

'That shop looks new,' she thought on her way back to the car, her arms laden with packages. A sign over the window, done in garish, hand-drawn letters, identified the shop as The Black Candle, with smaller lettering explaining that they specialized in the occult.

Peggy paused to glance in the display window. It was all tarot cards, candles of every size and description, Ouija boards, glass spheres that she decided must be intended as crystal balls; all a bit artificial and pretentious, but popular these days.

She was about to walk on when she looked beyond the display and saw Mrs. Denver talking with the salesgirl. It seemed to be a very intense conversation, and Peggy found herself remembering Mrs. Denver's interest in astrology. Probably she was guessing the girl's astrological sign and explaining how she knew.

Smiling to herself, Peggy went on to the car, piled the packages in the back seat, and drove to the market for groceries.

It was nearly noon by the time she headed home, the car now filled with bags and packages. The weather had turned warm and she was looking forward to dispensing with chores and enjoying her vacation. The boat, kept in storage, had been cleaned and serviced for them and was waiting at the dock. It would be a great afternoon for boating.

Her route actually took her past the boat landing, busy now with tourist traffic. She liked the bustle, the smell of fresh fish, and the roar of boats and voices and cars. She was sitting at a red light, savoring all the activity, when she suddenly saw Mrs. Denver again; and with her, of all people, Allison. The pair walked side by side, talking with their heads bent close. At that moment Allison seemed very engrossed in something Mrs. Denver was saying.

Peggy would have honked and tried to wave them over to the car, but at first she was too surprised at seeing Allison there, and by the time she had collected her wits, the light had changed. She drove off slowly, watching them in the rear-view mirror until they were out of sight.

She realized the incident troubled her out of all proportion. Of course it was a trivial thing. And she knew she was being unreasonable in having taken such an immediate dislike — no, distrust was more the word — to Mrs. Denver.

Why on earth, though, had Allison told her she wanted to do some things around the cottage if what she really intended to do was meet Mrs. Denver? It was not as if Allison had to have her permission to strike up a friendship. It seemed so . . . Peggy searched for the word . . . so sneaky.

On the other hand, she told herself, there was nothing to say Allison had actually intended meeting Mrs. Denver.

By the time Allison returned to the cottage, lunch was nearly ready. Peggy, working in the kitchen, heard the front screen door bang shut and made a mental note that they needed a new spring for it.

'Hi,' Allison said amiably, coming into the kitchen. She was dressed neatly — not as if she were just relaxing in a lake resort town, but dressed up. As if, Peggy found herself thinking, she'd had a business appointment.

'Hi yourself. I thought you were going to stick around here?'

'Oh, I was, but I got restless, so I decided to go for a stroll along the landing. It was kind of nice, really. I guess

I'd forgotten that Hunter's Point is such a pretty little town.'

Peggy, waiting for Allison to volunteer the information that she had run into Mrs. Denver, realized as the silence grew that it was not forthcoming. She almost asked, 'Meet anyone?', but checked herself at the last minute. Allison looked so happy, so recovered from her moods, that she hated to spoil it by sounding as though she'd been checking up on her.

'You know, I haven't been very good company so far,' Allison said, coming up behind her and putting an arm about Peggy's shoulders, 'and I am sorry, Peg. I promise you won't have to put up with any more of my bad moods.'

After that, Peggy could hardly ask her about Mrs. Denver.

2

They spent the afternoon on the lake and ate dinner that evening at the hotel again, at Allison's suggestion.

'After spending the afternoon out in the boat, I just can't see sweating over a hot stove,' was how she put it, although it was Peggy who did the cooking.

At first, Peggy had expected Mrs. Denver to show up 'spontaneously' at their table, but as the meal progressed and no one appeared, Peggy began to relax. For the first time this trip, she began to enjoy Allison's company.

'Something's certainly gotten into you,' she said over dessert. 'Ever since I picked you up at the airport you've been on a gloom trip, and today you're looking like the cat that swallowed the canary. How about telling me what's up?'

Allison smiled mysteriously. 'You wouldn't understand if I did.'

'Try me.'

'Mercury is in perigee.' Allison's eyes twinkled with a mischievous light. She looked all at once like the little girl who used to hide Peggy's dolls.

'Mercury . . . what on earth is that supposed to mean? Peri . . . what did you call it?'

Allison shrugged. 'I told you, you wouldn't understand it.'

'But . . . '

Allison laughed and pushed her chair back. 'Come on, let's stroll back to the house. I'm for calling it a night.'

'Already? But it's only eight-thirty. And anyway, I want to know what you mean about Mercury and whatever he's in.'

'It may only be eight-thirty but it's been a long, active day and I plan on hitting the sack. And as for the other, don't worry yourself about it, you'll understand better tomorrow.'

'Some sort of surprise, you mean?'

They came out of the restaurant onto the darkened street and turned in the direction of the cottage. 'Exactly,' Allison said.

Peggy stole a sideways glance at Allison.

She looked so keyed up, so exhilarated, that for a moment Peggy had a pang of doubt. There was so much she didn't know or understand about her sister. Was there some unsavory explanation for these sudden and drastic mood changes?

She resolved to be patient and wait until morning to learn what Allison's secret was. Whatever it was, it had certainly lifted Allison's spirits. Maybe it would do as much for hers.

The cottage was at the end of a shady street. There were other cottages along this way, but at this time only one other one, about half a block up from theirs, was occupied. A distorted rectangle of light spilled from its window across the sidewalk.

'I wonder who that is,' Peggy said.

'Who?'

'That car. It's a Rolls-Royce. Parked down by our place.' She nodded toward the large, silvery car parked — or so it seemed from that distance — directly in front of their cottage.

Allison shrugged. 'Probably another of the summer residents.'

'But none of the other cottages is opened up yet . . . oh, it's leaving.'

As she spoke, the Rolls began to glide silently away from the curb, in their direction. When it passed them, Peggy did a double-take. She'd had only a quick glimpse of the driver before he had turned his head away from her, but she would have sworn it was Mrs. Denver's chauffeur — what had his name been, Waldo? And that shadowy figure in the rear seat, leaning far back into the corner — had that been . . . ?

'Did you recognize them?' she asked.

'Who?' Allison gave her a blank look.

'In that car, the Rolls. I would have sworn it was Waldo and Mrs. Denver.'

'I didn't see them. But maybe it was. Maybe Mrs. Denver got lonesome for some company and decided to look us up. From the way she talked I got the feeling she doesn't know anyone here, and I'd say she's the sort who is a bit shy about meeting people.'

'I would have said she was rather forward about meeting people,' Peggy disagreed, remembering the way Mrs.

Denver had joined them at their table the night before. 'And anyway, they just drove right by us. If they had been looking for us, don't you think they would have recognized us?'

'Well, you're probably right. They couldn't have been looking for us or they'd have stopped when they saw us. When you get right down to it, it's kind of flattering ourselves to think she'd even remember us after one meeting, let alone look us up. She was probably trying to find someone else who lives down this way.'

'But — '

'Oh, look, Sis, why don't we just drop the subject?' Allison said sharply. Peggy was about to pursue it, but changed her mind and restrained her questions. She didn't want to spoil Allison's good mood now that she was finally perking up.

Maybe Mrs. Denver had something to do with Allison's surprise for the morning, and that was why Allison was being so mysterious and secretive. Yes, now that she thought of it, that was a likely explanation. Maybe Mrs. Denver had delivered something for Allison while they were out, something Allison didn't want Peggy to see yet — although certainly Mrs. Denver was the most unlikely delivery person Peggy could think of.

'I suppose you're right,' she said, impulsively linking her arm through Allison's as they crossed the street, but she couldn't resist a quick glance over her shoulder. The street was now silently empty, and not even the purr of a distant motor could be heard to prove that a car had ever been there.

★   ★   ★

It was the sound of a car that roused Peggy from sleep much later, in the middle of the night. She lay awake for some minutes, staring up at the ceiling. Something had awakened her, she couldn't say with certainty exactly what. A door closing? She had been lying there listening for a repetition of it, wondering if she should get up and go investigate. She heard nothing for several minutes; and then, faintly, the sound of a car door, and an engine coming to life.

She kicked back the light blanket and got out of bed, the floor cold on her bare feet. The bedrooms were in the rear, looking down toward the lake. The living room and kitchen were on the street side of the building, so she had to walk the width of the house to reach one of the windows looking out onto the road.

By that time, the car she'd heard was gone. She had just a glimpse of red taillights disappearing in the distance.

'Some kids, out parking,' she told herself, letting the curtains flutter closed. Still, she felt a strange prickling of uneasiness. Certain she would not quickly go back to sleep, she went into the kitchen and poured herself a glass of milk.

She was seated at the kitchen table, sipping it and feeling wide awake, when the rain began to fall, a gentle tapping at the window. Remembering the open window next to her bed, she hurried back to her bedroom to close it.

'I might as well get Allison's too,' she told herself, and stole into Allison's room on tiptoe.

She had closed the window, and was

almost to the hall again when she sensed something odd about Allison's room.

'Allison?' she whispered. There was no response. She went quietly closer to the bed.

It was empty.

'Allison?' She flicked on the lamp beside the bed, blinking in its sudden glare, and looked around. Allison was not in the room. 'Where are you?' she called more loudly.

She went through the cottage room by room, turning on lights, and as she went her uneasiness of a few minutes earlier began to grow into genuine anxiety. The clock on the kitchen wall informed her it was ten minutes to four in the morning. Where on earth could Allison be at that hour?

She thought then of the car she had heard. What if it had been her car? She hurried to the door that connected kitchen with garage. No, the Jag was just where she had left it. Anyway, she ought to have known it wasn't the Jag, it would have made a great deal more noise. The one she'd heard had been very quiet: a purr, almost. Like a Rolls-Royce — that thought came unbidden to her mind.

'Wait a minute, let's not panic,' she said aloud. Her voice sounded odd in the predawn stillness of the empty cottage. There could be all sorts of explanations for Allison's absence.

She made herself a cup of tea and sat in the kitchen sipping it thoughtfully, trying not to glance at the clock every minute or two. Finally, thinking that if Allison should come in she might think Peggy was waiting up to check on her, she went back to her bedroom and crawled into bed.

Maybe, she reasoned, Allison had met a boy and made a date . . . but so late? And why make a secret of it? Certainly she knew Peggy wouldn't object to her dating.

Or did she know that? Perhaps she really had gotten the idea that she was being punished, and that part of the punishment was a restriction of her freedom.

'I'll have to straighten that out in the morning,' Peggy told herself firmly. If — and she was immediately sorry she had let this thought into her consciousness — if Allison were home in the morning.

* * *

Allison was not home by morning, and Peggy, weary from lack of sleep and from worrying, made another discovery that had been overlooked during the night.

Not only was Allison gone, but all her belongings were gone too. Her closet and dresser were empty, her bags missing. There wasn't a trace of her in the room or, but for an empty coffee cup on the kitchen counter, anywhere in the cottage.

Peggy made herself coffee and sat, deliberately contemplating the singular situation in which she found herself. Where, she asked herself again and again, had Allison gone? And why?

Aside from her sulks at the beginning, there was no reason for her simply to disappear, and by yesterday she had seemed to work herself out of her bad mood. She had been great fun yesterday on the boat, and again at dinner last night. The only time she had shown any irritation had been on their way home, when Peggy thought she had seen Mrs. Denver, in that car.

At once her thoughts went to the wee hours, to the sound of a car door closing and the quiet murmur of an engine. She was sure Mrs. Denver had been parked outside the cottage earlier in the evening. And Mrs. Denver had joined them at the dinner table the night before, thrusting herself into their lives. She thought of Mrs. Denver mysteriously meeting Allison during the afternoon, a meeting Allison had neglected to mention.

Peggy could not shake her growing conviction that Mrs. Denver was the key to Allison's sudden disappearance. She was certain Mrs. Denver was with Allison; or if she wasn't, that she would know where Allison was.

Peggy pushed aside her half-finished cup of coffee and, dressing hurriedly, left for the police station downtown.

★ ★ ★

The officer she talked to, however, did not seem particularly impressed with Allison's vanishing. He filled out a report, asking Peggy questions in what seemed to her an uninterested voice.

'The missing girl, she's your sister, you say?' His pen moved rapidly over the official-looking paper.

'Yes. Adopted sister, actually.' She wished he would look up at her, show some concern or sympathy; anything but this complete lack of interest.

'And she ran off, you think?'

'I don't . . . no, I don't think she just 'ran off' — I don't know what happened to her. That's what I want you to find out.'

He did look up then, studying her in a business-like way. 'How old is your sister? Excuse me, your adopted sister?'

'She's nineteen.'

He put his pen down and leaned back in his chair, folding his hands in front of him. 'You understand, legally this girl is an adult. She can come and go as she pleases.'

Peggy took a deep breath. This man annoyed her. He was so unconcerned, so stickling, when all the while Allison was . . . whatever Allison was. 'Yes, of course I understand that, but if she didn't go of her own accord . . . ?'

That roused him a little. He leaned forward again, but he did not pick up his pen. 'You think there's something fishy about her leaving?'

She managed a bit of a smile for the officer, for the first time since she had come in. Finally she had his attention. 'Yes, I do,' she said firmly.

'This room she left, was there any sign of a struggle?'

'Why, no, but . . . ' She had lost him again. He leaned back, the chair squeaking. 'I can't imagine she would just voluntarily sneak away in the middle of the night. As you said, she is an adult, there would be no reason to steal away like that. If she wanted to go, there was nothing to prevent it.'

He narrowed his eyes. 'You two had any kind of quarrel?'

She hesitated, but she saw from his expression that he had already made note of her reaction to the question, and answered it for himself.

'Not a quarrel, no, not exactly.' He looked dubious, and she hastened to explain. 'There was some friction, earlier, but it was all patched up. Really, it was. She was fine yesterday.'

He nodded his head knowingly. She felt like stamping her foot or shouting, anything to get through to him. 'And she gave you no clue that anything was going to happen, that she had anything in mind?'

Like an unwelcome guest, the memory came back to her. In all her concern she had forgotten it until now. Her face reddened as she said, 'Well, she did say she had a surprise for me, for this morning. But I'm sure she didn't mean . . . ' She stopped. As she had realized he would, he had already drawn his own conclusions. He spread his hands out flat.

'There you have it. Her surprise was that she had some plans of her own. Maybe she eloped.'

'By herself? She didn't know anyone here.'

He went on, oblivious to her interruption. 'You told me earlier, you'd seen her talking to some woman — Denver, was that it? Maybe she had more friends around here than you knew. Maybe a boyfriend followed her up here from school. Maybe she just felt like being by herself for a while.'

Angrily, Peggy said, 'In other words, you don't intend to do anything to find her?'

He sighed. 'Miss, there is nothing I can do. A young woman of legal age decides to leave, there's no evidence of a struggle; apparently she left of her own volition. It happens all the time. Look, I'll tell you what: if it'll make you happier, I'll send someone around to the cottage, to have a look-see. Maybe — I doubt it, but just maybe — your sister was taken against her will, and someone took the time to straighten things up neatly. You have to admit, it sounds unlikely, with you sleeping in the next room, but I'll have one of our men check it out, okay?'

'And in the meantime, there's no way you can look for her? She is a missing person, isn't she?'

'Well, no, not according to the law, not until she's been missing for twenty-four hours. If you want to come back tomorrow and file a missing persons report . . . ' His shrug said he didn't think it would be worth her while.

Peggy bit her lip in frustration. She tried to think of something she could say that would change his mind. Finally, unable to think of anything more, she turned on her heel and started away.

'Miss, take my advice, don't worry about it,' he called after her. 'I'd be willing to bet money that by this time tomorrow you'll know where she is.'

She paused to look over her shoulder. 'That might not necessarily be a blessing,' she said.

Outside the station, she hesitated indecisively. Of course, there was always the possibility that he was right, that Allison had gone freely. Not to elope, certainly there would have been some clue or hint of that. A joke, perhaps? Her sense of humor was sometimes thoughtless.

What was it she had said last night? Mercury was in . . . She searched for the word. Mercury was in perigee. What on earth could that mean? It sounded like astrology. Mercury was a planet, and she vaguely thought she recalled one of her girlfriends, who went in for astrology, talking about Mercury in her horoscope.

Astrology brought her right back to Mrs. Denver. Peggy was more convinced than ever that Mrs. Denver was the key to the mystery. She glanced down the street. The hotel was only a few blocks from here. Had Mrs. Denver said she was staying at the hotel, or had she only been there that evening for cocktails? She couldn't remember.

Anything, however, was better than doing nothing. She walked to the hotel. The desk clerk knew her, which made her task a bit easier, but not much more fruitful.

'Mrs. Denver? Yes, she was here, but she checked out this morning,' he told her. 'During the night, actually. I came on at five, and it was before then. Unusual time to check out. She must have had a long trip ahead of her.'

'Or some other reason for such an odd hour.' Peggy was not at all surprised that Mrs. Denver had disappeared along with

Allison. 'Look, do you have an address for her, a home address?'

He looked embarrassed. 'I'm sorry, I'm afraid we're not allowed to give out that information. You can understand. Invasion of privacy, that sort of thing.'

'Yes, of course,' she said, disappointed.

★ ★ ★

She was almost back to her car when she passed the shop she had noticed the day before, The Black Candle. She paused to look inside. A young woman with a long ponytail was just opening up for the day. On an impulse, Peggy went inside.

'Hello, can I help you?' The saleswoman gave her a friendly smile.

'Perhaps,' Peggy began, feeling a little foolish. 'I . . . I'm looking for someone. I thought you might have some idea where I could find her.'

The girl shrugged. Her expression said, 'This isn't going to make me any money,' but she was polite enough. 'I'm new in town. I'm afraid I don't know very many people around here. What was the name?'

'Her name is Denver, Mrs. Denver. She's an older woman, fifty or so, I should say, with silver-gray hair, and she's very knowledgeable about astrology. I saw her in here yesterday talking to you.'

'Yes, she didn't give me her name, but I do remember a woman who looked like that. She stopped by in the morning.' Her eyes narrowed suspiciously. 'What did you say you want to find her for?'

'I . . . we shared a table at the restaurant last night and she gave me a lift home afterwards,' Peggy said, 'but I seem to have left my sweater in her car. It's an expensive sweater, you see, cashmere, but I couldn't remember where she said she was staying, and when I passed by just now I remember seeing her here yester-day. She didn't say where she was from or anything like that, did she?'

'No, but you can make a swap if you want, because she left something here.' She went behind the counter and reached down, bringing up a cigarette case and a book of matches. 'Not exactly a cashmere sweater, but I suppose it'll make up a little for the loss. Anyway, I don't smoke, so you may as well have them.'

'Oh, thank you.' Peggy took the case and the matches from her. 'Maybe I can find her and return these — and get my sweater back.'

'Good luck, but I don't think she was from around here.'

Peggy wasn't listening. She was staring down at the items in her hand. The cigarette case was an expensive one, alligator trimmed in gold, but it was the matches that really interested her. They had come from a bank in Ives. Ives Point was near Sandusky along the lake shore, and the heart of Ohio's grape-growing region. The Ives ferry carried passengers to the offshore islands — Middle Bass, Put-in-Bay, and several smaller, privately owned islands — on which were the chief vineyards and wineries of the area.

She turned the matchbook over in her hand. She had worked briefly as a bank teller, and in her experience, banks often printed their advertising on matchbooks, but they did not as a rule distribute them anywhere but in their own banks. If Mrs. Denver had these matches in her

45

possession, most likely she had either gotten them from someone who had been in that bank, or she had been in the bank herself.

A customer had come into the shop and the clerk was now busy with her. Thinking of something else she wanted to ask, Peggy lingered, waiting for her to be free again. She strolled around, looking at the merchandise. A series of books devoted to astrology filled a small rack, one book for each of the twelve zodiac signs. On an impulse, she picked up the book on Leo and skimmed through its pages.

'The Leo woman is vain, egotistical,' she read. 'Somewhat lazy at times . . . graceful but leisurely in movement, vulnerable to flattery. She tends to have dark eyes and full, flowing hair. Vanity is the key . . . '

'What nonsense,' she thought, making to replace the book on the rack. Then she had the thought that she should buy something to make up for using so much of the clerk's time, and retrieved the astrology book.

The clerk was free now. Peggy walked over to where she stood behind the counter and lay the book down, with the money to cover its cost.

'I wonder . . . ' she said as the young woman rang up the sale. 'You seem to know astrology, could you help me with something?'

'I'll try, but I'm not in the same class as your friend. She was uncanny. I would have liked her to cast my chart.'

'If someone said to you, 'Mercury is in perigee' — I think that's the right phrase, but I'm not certain — what would it mean?'

The clerk frowned as she put the book and the sales slip into a bag. 'Well, I'm not sure exactly. Perigee is an astronomical term, it means a planet or a heavenly body is at is closest point to the other. In other words, Mercury is as close to Earth as it ever gets.'

'Yes, but what does that mean astrologically? Does it have any special significance?'

'I don't know specifically about Mercury, but when a planet is closest to Earth, in perigee, it means that it has its strongest influence. And Mercury . . . let me see . . . Mercury is an important body. It influences moods, for one thing. You know, people who have wild ups and then wild downs. Mercury moods, a friend of mine calls them, and does he ever suffer from them. You never know what he's going to do next.

'I guess if Mercury was in perigee, he'd be likely to do anything. You know, jump from the Empire State Building, race a train, wrestle tigers. It's an energy sign, for one thing, and a sign of variety. Is your friend a Gemini? They're awfully influenced by Mercury. And another thing, Mercury people are influenced by the people around them. And they desire change. Does any of that help?'

'I'm not sure. Let me see if I understand — you mean that if Mercury is in perigee, all of these influences would be heightened, is that right?'

'Exactly. Anybody who's a Mercury person would be just . . . like, spaced out, if you know what I mean. They're liable to jump at just any hare-brained idea.'

Peggy smiled wryly and nodded. 'Yes, I think that about covers it. Thanks again.'

'Any time.' The clerk's quick, shallow smile slid from Peggy to a new customer who had just entered the shop. This time Peggy left. She retrieved her car from the station and drove thoughtfully home to the cottage, and let herself in.

Mercury in perigee. Allison, looking like the cat who had swallowed the canary, and then disappearing during the night, not a word, not a trace. Had Allison dropped this teasing morsel as an explanation, or a clue? What could it possibly mean? Was she off on some lark? Or was she in some kind of trouble?

'And what do I do about the folks?' Peggy wondered aloud, once more surveying Allison's empty room.

She dreaded the thought of calling home and informing them of yet another problem with Allison. Her father had warned her that he was at the end of his patience with Allison's antics. Even if this proved to be some sort of innocent escapade, it just might be the straw to break the camel's back.

'But what if it isn't innocent?' That was the question that haunted her. Allison was impulsive, quick to jump into things — often foolish, even dangerous things. What kind of situation might she have gotten into now?

One thing she was sure of — Mrs. Denver was no foolish schoolgirl. Whatever Mrs. Denver might be involved in, it was almost certainly deadly serious.

She took the cigarette case and matchbook from her pocket and regarded them briefly. Ives. An hour's drive along the lake. Of course, there was no assurance she would be able to find Allison, or even Mrs. Denver, there. She had only a book of matches to hint that either of them had even gone in that direction.

On the other hand, it was the only clue she had. She went into her bedroom and began tossing things into an overnight bag.

3

Not much of a clue, she thought later, looking from the matchbook to the ferry that carried cars and passengers from Ives Point to Put-in-Bay. The next boat left at 2:45, thirty minutes from now, and within fifteen minutes she must decide whether to add her car to the already growing line of waiting vehicles. From Ives Point the ferry made a fifteen-minute trip to the Lime Kiln Docks; and from there, so she had been informed, it was just a mile and a half into the main part of town at Put-in-Bay.

But exactly what, she wondered, would she accomplish by arriving at the main part of town? Or, for that matter, what had she accomplished by coming this far?

She had found the bank from which the matches had come, but once there she found herself at a dead end. She had even talked to a teller, who knew no one named Denver and who had explained she was not at liberty to give out information regarding customers, although she was persuaded — perhaps by Peggy's expression of profound innocence — to check. Alas, there was no Denver account on file.

Short of waiting in the bank's lobby for days until — and if — Mrs. Denver showed up, there seemed really nothing more Peggy could do.

She dropped onto a wooden bench next to the sidewalk. It was no use; she might as well go back to Hunter's Point and call the family. Maybe they could suggest a next step. At least she wouldn't feel so alone in this.

It was at this low point in her spirits that chance favored her. She glanced toward the ferry, still trying to make up her mind whether to take the trip across to Put-in-Bay, and saw a familiar, hulking figure — Waldo, Mrs. Denver's chauffeur, walking rapidly along the boat landing.

Her heart leapt. Then she had been right in letting the matchbook lead her here. If Waldo was here, could Mrs. Denver be far behind?

She jumped up and started after him,

but the traffic held her back; and by the time she had crossed the street to where she had seen him, he was gone from sight. This was a popular tourist point and there were crowds of people everywhere, some waiting for the ferry, others just strolling about.

She hurried along in the direction he had been going, looking right and left. But there was no sight of him anywhere.

All around her were people, movements, the sights and sounds and smells of a boat landing. Gulls wheeled and cried; children yelled; somewhere nearby an engine sprang to life.

She turned to retrace her steps. As she did so, a boat slipped from its moorings. The movement caught her eye and she turned toward it in time to see the brutish Waldo at the wheel of a powerful inboard cruiser. As she watched, the boat accelerated, its nose lifting slightly, and pulled away from the landing.

She walked to the dock where it had been moored, staring after it in frustration as, its speed increasing, it shrank in the distance. An old man who had been fishing from the dock nearby was in the act of gathering up his things. He had the look of a local rather than a tourist, and on impulse she approached him.

'Excuse me,' she said, giving him a hopeful smile, 'do you know that boat that just left?'

He glanced over the water briefly, then back at her. 'Reckon I do,' he said laconically.

'Can you tell me who it belongs to?'

'Belongs to the Lions family. This is their dock. What do you want to know for?'

'I . . . I thought I knew the man who was driving it just now.' She tried to make her inquiries sound casual, not too concerned, but hope was rising like a mountain spring within her.

'That'd be Waldo.'

'Yes, that's him.' She was unable to keep from sounding pleased. 'Where could I find him if I wanted to see him again?'

His look questioned why anyone would want to see Waldo again, but he simply said, 'He works for the family. Reckon

54

you'd have to go there.' He nodded his head toward the lake.

'They live on the lake somewhere?'

'Not *on* it; *in* it, so to speak. Lions Island, straight out there, beyond Sugar and Rattlesnake Islands. It's where the wine is made.'

The name registered with her then: Lions. The House of Lions, Ohio's premier wine. She had read of their island vineyards, producing supposedly the finest Catawba grapes in the country.

'Of course, how stupid of me,' she murmured. 'Is the island on one of the tours?'

He snorted at the foolishness of her question. 'Lions Island? Not likely. They don't encourage any kind of visitors. Afraid someone would step on a grape, mostly likely. Look, little lady, I don't know what your interest in the Lionses is, but if I was you, I'd forget it. The last fellow tried to visit out there got thrown into the lake, clothes and all, like to drown before he got to his boat.

'Why don't you take one of the regular tours? There's plenty of wineries you can visit with no trouble, and forget you ever saw this Waldo fellow. Maybe it ain't for me to say, but that one's a mean customer. He ain't for the likes of you.'

Peggy stared out over the water. A boy nearby had thrown a stone into it, and circles radiated out from the spot where the stone had splashed into the lake. Her thoughts swirled in similar circles. Waldo. Allison. Mrs. Denver. A mysterious island out there in the lake, a famed family of vintners. She did not understand how but she was sure that, like the circles in the water, they all came back to some central point. Like a siren's song, Lions Island called to her.

'Is there somewhere I can hire a boat?' she asked.

The old man's eyes said it all. He knew her for a fool. But after a moment he shrugged and said, 'Old George, two docks down, he's got the best ones to rent.' He collected his gear and, plainly dismissing her and her problems from his mind, shuffled away, shaking his head.

★ ★ ★

The island lay like a green cloud on the watery horizon. It had been easy to find with Old George's directions, although he too had regarded her as if she were crazy, and had demanded twice the usual deposit on the boat. 'Never know if I'm going to get it back, you going out there,' he said.

'But why? What's the big bugaboo about going to Lions Island?'

He was no more informative than the fisherman had been, though. 'They don't like visitors,' was all he said.

'Well, you don't have to worry about your boat. I'm quite used to handling one and I promise I only intend to see someone at the house and talk to them a few minutes.'

'You'll never get past the gates. No one ever does. Guarded by lions, they say.'

She had felt a shiver of apprehension. 'Lions? You mean real ones? Surely they don't have dangerous animals roaming loose on the island?'

He fixed his eyes on hers and said, 'Take my advice, head for Put-in-Bay, have yourself something to eat — try

Daisy's, it ain't much to look at but the food's damned good — and then head back here.'

* * *

The island grew larger until its features were distinct. It was so little known or publicized that in her mind she had pictured it as small, but now she could see it was not. It looked as big as the larger islands in the chain.

She could make out the slopes, planted with vines; and in the distance, apparently on the middle of the island, the house itself, a grand old manor looking not unlike a French chateau. Around it all, encircling the entire island as nearly as she could tell, was a forbidding stone wall. She reflected on the work that must have gone into transporting all that stone to an island in the middle of a lake. Even from the first, the Lions family must have valued their privacy very highly.

She spotted a landing, with a boathouse as elegant-looking as many fine homes. She headed for it, cutting back the engine.

It was foolish to suppose she could just arrive and stroll up to the house unnoticed, but she felt an instinctive urge to be as quiet about her coming as possible.

As it was, no one seemed to notice her as she landed. She docked, tied up the boat, and scrambled up onto the dock. Still she saw no one. In the boathouse she had a glimpse of the cruiser she had seen Waldo piloting.

The stone wall came almost down to the dock and there, directly before her, was a great iron gate barring her way. Of course, treasuring their isolation as they did, the Lions would not have left it possible for anyone who did stop uninvited at their dock to simply climb up to their house.

There must surely be some way for visitors to announce themselves. She walked closer to the gate and saw a bell, but did not ring it at once. Beyond the gates a gravel drive cut through a cultivated forest. The wall was too high for her to see over, and the trees effectively hid the house from any curious eyes.

It was then she saw the lions. Massive iron beasts that seemed poised to strike.

This was the moment that was to trouble Peggy again and again, as if in a constantly recurring dream. Where was Allison? Was she behind the grim, forbidding gate of the lions? Or was this only a wild goose chase?

Peggy stared at the enormous iron lions crouched on either side, guarding the gates of the estate. Lions were her symbol; the symbol, she'd learned from her astrology book, of the astrological sign Leo.

These lions, though, were not the warm, friendly lions pictured in the book. They were fierce and angry-looking, and they seemed to issue a warning of violence and tragedy to anyone who dared challenge them. They intimidated nearly as effectively as living lions would have done.

She reached out a hand to the wrought iron of one of the gates, and to her surprise it swung inward. It was not locked after all. Perhaps the owners thought the sight of their massive structure and their leonine guards were enough to discourage trespassers.

Under most circumstances, Peggy thought, they would be. For a moment, no more, she hesitated. Then she passed through, casting an apprehensive glance at the inscription above, carved into the stone in letters so bold they seemed almost to speak their warning aloud: *Beware, we stand at the gates of hell.*

She was inside, standing in the drive that led through the trees. Did the family drive from house to dock? She had estimated the island's width at somewhere near two miles, maybe more. It couldn't be a long walk from here to the house.

A sudden sound in the shrubbery to her right made her start. She turned and to her amazement, there was Allison, the leaves of a tree casting shadows across her pale face — but it was Allison, unmistakably Allison. A flood of relief washed over Peggy.

'Allison, thank God I've found you,' Peggy cried. 'What on earth happened to you? I've been looking everywhere for you.'

'Who are you?' Allison asked.

Peggy stood stunned into silence, unable to believe what she had heard. She stared at the young woman before her. It was Allison's face, Allison's expression, Allison's voice. But it was the soul of a stranger who was saying, 'Who are you, what are you doing here? This is private property, you know. We don't allow trespassers.'

4

Peggy, still speechless, could only stare at the angry-looking person before her. She even doubted her own senses. Could she have made a mistake? Was it only someone who looked like Allison, a resemblance magnified by her concern for her missing sister?

She was certain she had never seen Allison in that outfit — jodhpurs, a silk blouse that most certainly came straight from Paris, a Hermes scarf. She looked elegant, poised, the mistress of her world.

Peggy shook her head as if to rearrange her confusing thoughts. No, it had to be Allison. There couldn't be two people who looked that much alike, even down to Allison's way of cocking her head slightly to the side when she looked directly at you.

'Why are you staring at me like that?' Allison demanded. 'And why haven't you answered any of my questions? You'd better talk fast before I summon the servants and have you thrown back into the lake.'

Her cold arrogance finally penetrated Peggy's confusion. Anger replaced her bewilderment. She'd been through a dreadful scare. Her holiday had been ruined. She'd had to boat out to this island, only to find Allison apparently caught up in some weird drama of her own making — and treating her as though she were a criminal.

'How dare you?' she said angrily, taking a step closer to Allison. 'After all you've put me through, I ought to grab you and shake a little sense into you. Of all the stupid things you've ever done, this is far and away the most — '

'What's going on here?'

Peggy nearly jumped a foot off the ground. She'd been so excited about finding Allison, and then so angry at her behavior, that she had been unaware anyone else was approaching down the gravel drive. She turned to find a man standing directly behind her, and he looked no more friendly or welcoming than her sister.

'What is this all about?' he demanded,

fixing steel-gray eyes on Peggy. They were cold eyes, and hard. One could not imagine them ever lighting up with pleasure or happiness. Certainly not with kindness or love.

He was handsome, though, tall and lean. His mouth was a cruel and sensuous line, his dark hair spilling in undisciplined curls across his bronze forehead.

'A trespasser, Alex,' Allison said. 'I found her sneaking around down here and ordered her off the island, but she refuses to leave.'

'Sneaking around? Of all the . . . ' Peggy was nearly livid by now.

'I'll take care of this,' the man called Alex said. 'You'd better go back up to the house.'

Allison's glance flickered over Peggy and back to him. She nodded and started wordlessly past Peggy. Peggy reached out to grab her wrist.

'Now wait just a minute,' she said, 'you listen to me — '

'No, you listen to *me*.' The man's powerful fingers closed over Peggy's hand. She let go of Allison who, without hesitation, hurried away in the direction of the house. Peggy found herself held firmly in place, not only by the grip of his hand on hers, but by the icy stare of his eyes.

'This is private property.' He spoke slowly but firmly, enunciating each word with exaggerated precision. 'We don't take kindly to strangers poking around. Now I would suggest you get back into your boat and head for the mainland, or Put-in-Bay, or wherever you were headed. And don't come back here.'

'This may be private property,' Peggy responded heatedly, 'but that woman is my sister and I do not intend to leave until I find out what you've done to her to make her behave like that.'

'Your what?' He laughed then, but it was not a warm laugh, nor did it do anything to lessen the tension. 'I see.'

'No, I don't think you do.'

'I see that you are either a practical joker or up to some sort of stunt, or maybe you are completely mad. In any case, I must insist again that you leave.' He did not wait for her to agree but, holding firmly to her hand, fairly dragged her through the gate toward the landing where her boat was tied up.

'Where is Mrs. Denver?' Peggy asked. 'I know she's here too. I demand to speak to her.'

They had reached the landing. He let go her wrist and stepped back a pace from her. 'There is no one here by that name,' he said.

'Then tell Allison — '

'Nor by that name either.'

'I don't care what name she's using, I want to talk to her.'

She moved as if she would go by him, but he stepped into her path, and his manner was so menacing that for the first time since he had appeared on the scene, she felt a twinge of fear.

'My dear young lady,' he said, and now his voice was so low that it did indeed sound ominous, 'so far I have tried to treat you as reasonably as possible under the circumstances, but I can assure you we have treated other trespassers and troublemakers with much less gentleness, and you have made a nuisance of yourself. Now, I will tell you for the last time, get off this island.'

Peggy tried to meet his angry gaze, but she saw that he was prepared to back up his threats. Fearful of what he might do, she backed down. With a last glance at the imposing lions' gate, she clambered down into the boat.

He came to untie the lines while she started the engine. His nearness gave her a sense of alarm. She half-expected him to change his mind after all and throw her into the drink. Certainly he looked strong enough, and mean enough, to do just that, and she was glad when the boat began to slowly move away from the dock.

He watched her go, standing on the dock with his arms folded across his chest. She had toyed with the idea that perhaps she could only pretend to leave, and circle back when he had gone, but apparently he was not going to give her any such opportunity. He gave no sign of budging until she was well out of sight.

With a sigh of frustration, she pushed her hair back from her face and headed the boat toward Ives Point. Her thoughts seethed and churned as violently as the water in her wake.

What on earth had Allison gotten herself into now? That was the crucial question. Why had she pretended she didn't know Peggy, and that she wasn't Allison? What hold did these people, strangers until two days ago, have over her that they could force her to run away with them in the middle of the night, to that strange island house; to pretend she was not even herself, and deny recognition to the person supposedly closest to her in the world?

That thought brought her up short. Was she the closest person to Allison in the world? Apparently not, or Allison would not have denied her just now.

Unless she was in danger, unless she was afraid to admit the truth. Maybe she had known that man was close enough to hear. Perhaps she hadn't dared speak frankly for fear of the consequences. But what consequences?

Yet, she had to admit to herself, Allison hadn't looked afraid. She'd looked angry, and very much at home there, confident of herself and, yes, even haughty.

For the first time, Peggy realized that she didn't really know her adopted sister very well at all.

* * *

The Sheriff to whom Peggy spoke in Ives Point was polite but no more sympathetic than the policeman in Hunger's Point had been.

'Look, Miss Conners, I'd like to help you, but I don't see exactly what it is you expect of the law. The young woman, your sister, you say she's legally of age, you say you talked to her on Lions Island, that she was moving about freely, not as if she were a prisoner or anything like that — which, believe me, knowing the Lions family, would be pretty hard to put stock in anyway. It sounds to me like she's just decided to go there of her own volition, and there's not much you or I can do about it.'

He folded his hands in his lap, and stared at her in a friendly but not very encouraging way.

'But I don't believe she did go there of her own volition. And I don't believe she's staying there of her own volition either. I'm sure there's something terribly wrong here, something involving my sister, and I mean to find out what it is. If you can't or won't help me, I'll find out for myself.'

'Miss, the Lions family has been here for generations. They are very important people to this community and they enjoy a fine reputation.'

'In other words, you're afraid to question them for fear of consequences. Right by might, is that what you're telling me?'

He met her gaze evenly and there was a glint of anger in his eyes. Finally, after a lengthy pause, he said, 'All right, have it your way. I'll go out to Lions Island and see if they can shed any light on things.'

'I'll go with you,' Peggy said, springing to her feet. For a moment she thought he would veto this suggestion but, with another cold look at her, he nodded, and she followed him from his office.

Lions Island looked no less ominous to her this time, even though she was in the company of the Sheriff and two members of the Lake Patrol. The island still seemed to draw in on itself as they approached. It was evening by now, and the lake mist had begun to hang about the stone wall and the distant roof of the chateau. Peggy thought how total the night-time would be out here, away from city lights and city sounds. Was Allison frightened here at night?

The boat slowed, and in a few minutes they were clambering onto the landing. As they did so, Peggy saw a man approaching. At first she thought it was the same man she had met earlier and, despite the three men with her, she felt a twinge of fear.

As the man came closer, however, she saw she was mistaken. She had never seen this man before. He had a resemblance to the other, but he was thinner. He was handsome, too, in much the same way, but he had a taut, whip-like quality about him, as if he were tensed for some sort of violent action. Despite the fading of the daylight, he wore sunglasses that made it hard to read his expression.

'Evening, Jack,' the Sheriff greeted him.

'Sheriff, boys.' Jack nodded and his eyes went from the men to Peggy, but unlike the man she'd met on her first visit, he gave her a friendly smile. 'What can I do for you?'

Peggy started to answer but the Sheriff cut her off. 'This young lady seems to think you've got her sister a prisoner here.'

Jack's eyebrows shot up and he allowed himself a faint chuckle. 'Well, one hardly knows what to say. The last time I looked, the dungeons were empty. But you're welcome to come have a look, if you like.'

'I think I should, Jack. You boys wait here, this won't take long.'

'I'll come with you,' Peggy said.

'You'll wait here,' the Sheriff said in a voice that brooked no argument. 'You boys see that this young lady doesn't go wandering off anyplace on her own.'

She watched the Sheriff and Jack pass

through the lion gate and start up the gravel drive. She had a sense of renewed frustration, but at least the Sheriff would see Allison. If Allison were simply afraid to admit who she was, she'd have no reason to hold back with the lawman right there. Whatever hold these people had on her, once she was out of danger, Allison would set things straight. Peggy was sure that in a few minutes she would see them coming back down the drive, Allison with the Sheriff.

She went along the dock and sat beside one of the pilings, leaning back against it, and watched the sun sinking into the distant water.

I'll be glad when this is all over, she thought with a weary sigh.

It was not to be over so quickly, though. When at last she saw the Sheriff once again pass through the lions' gate, he was accompanied not by Allison, but by the same smiling man as before, the one he had addressed as Jack. Peggy scrambled to her feet, brushed off her skirt, and started to meet them.

'Let's go,' the Sheriff greeted her

brusquely. He nodded to the lake patrolmen and they hurried to cast off the boat.

'But I don't understand,' Peggy said, looking from the lawman to Jack. 'Where's Allison?'

'That I can't tell you, miss, but I can tell you one thing, she's not here.'

'But that can't be. I saw her myself. Did you go everywhere, see everything?'

'I saw everything I needed to see. I saw old Jacob Lions, one of the nicest, most generous men this state has ever known, and I felt ashamed of myself, coming out here bothering folks. He's sick, miss, damned sick, that's why they don't want anyone hanging around making a big racket. That's why they didn't want you running all over the place hollering about your sister. They don't want him disturbed, and I don't blame them.'

She wilted under his barely controlled anger. 'I'm sorry,' she said meekly. 'Truly. But if he's ill, he might not know she's here. It wouldn't be his fault if he didn't.'

'It sure isn't. And as for his not knowing, let me tell you, I didn't just talk to him. I talked to Jack here, and his brother, and to their niece. I even talked to Jacob's financial advisor, who is visiting just now, and to one of the servants. Now, miss, it's just not conceivable that this sister of yours could be here, on this little island, and none of them know anything about it.'

'But . . . ' She wanted to say, 'They could be lying,' but she checked herself. She was aware that she was the center of attention, and none of it friendly. The Sheriff was angry, the lake patrolmen watching her with amusement. Only Jack Lions seemed sympathetic.

'It's all right, Sheriff,' he said. 'I can understand how the young lady feels. No doubt she's worried about her missing sister, and anxiety sometimes makes us jump to faulty conclusions.'

In the face of his kind voice and sympathetic manner, she felt foolish indeed. 'I'm sorry to have caused so much trouble,' she murmured, unable to meet his gentle gaze.

'It's just one of those Leo traits,' he said with a smile. 'Boldness in the cause of right. And I've no doubt you were convinced you were right.'

'I was, but it seems I was mistaken in my conviction.'

'If that's all settled, then, let's be shoving off,' the Sheriff said. 'It's getting dark and my wife's going to wonder what happened to me.' He jumped down into the boat.

Shamefacedly, she followed. Jack Lions came to help her into the boat, squeezing her hand and holding it a fraction of a second longer than was necessary. The patrolmen were quick to cast off and before she could take a seat in the rear of the boat, they were moving away from the dock.

She sat despondently by herself in the back, looking out over the now-dark water and wishing she could clear her mind of her confused and troubled thoughts. She had made a fool of herself. Worse, she had alienated the man she would have to ask to help her find Allison.

But I *have* found Allison, she thought stubbornly. I know where she is, I just don't know why she's there or why no one will admit she is Allison.

She remembered something then, and moved up the boat to put a cautious hand on the Sheriff's shoulder. He turned his head to glower at her.

'Sheriff, did you see Mrs. Denver?' she asked him.

'I asked. There's no one there by that name either.' They were shouting to make themselves heard over the roar of the boat. The town loomed up rapidly ahead of them, the nose of the boat lifting out of the water as it raced for home.

She made her way back to the rear of the boat and sat thinking. No Mrs. Denver either. That created another possibility, didn't it? That since her first visit, Mrs. Denver and Allison, knowing she was sure to be back with the authorities, had left. But where would they have gone next?

Or were they ever there? Everyone was so sure she was mistaken. Was it possible that in her anxiety over Allison, she had made such a mistake — as Jack had suggested?

Suddenly she saw him, smiling at her

sympathetically and saying, 'It's one of those Leo traits.'

How could he have known she was a Leo? No one had mentioned that, surely. But Mrs. Denver had known, and Allison. And they must have talked to him about her, discussed their 'problem' and how to cope with it.

They were back at the dock and the Sheriff was offering his hand to help her out of the boat. She took it and clambered onto the dock, but she stood with her shoulders firmly back, her chin up once more.

She had not been mistaken. Allison was there, or had been there, Allison and Mrs. Denver. Unwittingly, Jack had confirmed that for her, given her the proof that she was right and the Sheriff wrong. She knew she would never convince him of that, but in her own mind there was now complete certainty.

'Well, sorry I couldn't help you, miss,' the Sheriff said. 'I'd advise you to go back home and wait till you hear from your sister. It's my bet she'll show up.'

'Yes, I'm sure she will,' Peggy said.

'Good night, Sheriff.'

She walked away from him, not to head for home, as he had suggested, but to look for a hotel. She was sure as well that Allison would show up — right here, in this town.

She intended to be here when she did.

5

'Coffee, miss?'

Peggy started and glanced up at the young waitress beside her table. She had been far away, in a gloomy landscape of her own fears and concerns, most of them centered on Allison.

'Please,' Peggy said, managing a wan smile. She felt pale and drawn this morning, after a nearly sleepless night. For one thing, she'd had to call home once she checked into this motel, and tell her parents of Allison's mysterious disappearance and her subsequent strange behavior.

'But I don't understand,' her mother had said. 'If you've found Allison, isn't that the end of it? Let me talk to her, can you, I'll straighten her out in a hurry.'

Peggy had to explain patiently that Allison was not with her, and again that Allison insisted she was not Allison.

'I think you'd better come home,' was

her father's advice. 'Leave this business up to the authorities.'

'But the authorities aren't doing anything. They keep telling me that Allison left of her own free will and there's nothing they can do.'

'Then there's nothing you can do either.'

At length, she had persuaded them around to her view: that she would stay where she was for a few days, just until she had an opportunity to see Allison alone and get the truth out of her.

'Then I'll come home, with or without her,' she promised, and ended the conversation before they had an opportunity to insist otherwise.

Afterward, though, alone in the darkness of her motel room, she'd had to face the problem more squarely. She did not know how she was going to manage to see Allison again, especially alone. The stone beasts at the lion gate guarded her as effectively as if they were real animals. Allison was behind them, and with her the answers to all the maddening questions she had raised — but how to reach her?

'You must be the woman who's looking for her sister,' the waitress said, setting Peggy's breakfast in front of her.

Startled from her reverie, Peggy nearly knocked over her glass of orange juice. 'I beg your pardon?'

The waitress looked embarrassed. 'Gee, sorry, I didn't mean to stick my nose in. The Sheriff is my uncle, and he was over for a barbecue last night, so we got the whole story. It's a drag, isn't it?'

'I'll say,' Peggy murmured; and then, more interestedly, 'Do you know the Lions family?'

'Me?' She looked astonished at the suggestion. 'Gosh, hardly, they're not in my class, if you know what I mean.'

'But you do know of them?'

The waitress glanced over her shoulder. Only one other table was occupied and another waitress was tending to those customers. 'Oh, sure, I know who they are, and stuff like that. But they don't exactly mingle here in town, they stick to themselves. I guess you noticed that.'

'I got that impression. How many of them are there, by the way?'

'Mmm, let me see. Old Jacob Lions, of course; he was head of the clan, so to speak, but I hear he's pretty sick these days. His wife died years ago, but she was nice, as I remember, friendlier than the rest of them, at least to me. Of course, I was just a little girl then.'

'He has only the two sons?'

'Just one, Alex. Jack is a kind of cousin or something. No one knows much about him. He doesn't come into town very often. When he does, he has an eye for the ladies, I think.'

'And Alex is stand-offish?'

The waitress shrugged and glanced around the shop again. 'Actually, he hasn't been around here much either. He was living in France. The family has some wine properties there too, I hear. He just came home a few days ago.'

'And there's a girl too, right?'

'That's Melissa, old Jacob's granddaughter. She just came back too.'

Peggy started to ask something more, but the waitress said, 'Excuse me,' and went to greet a couple who had just come in.

Waiting impatiently for her to finish with

her new customers, Peggy felt the first stirrings of hope since she had gotten up that morning. A granddaughter who had been away and recently returned, and Allison just arriving here. Something, she thought, that may be the missing link in the chain: a link between Melissa and Allison.

It was ten minutes before the waitress returned to her table, bearing a coffeepot. She refilled the cup and would have gone, but Peggy stopped her with another question.

'This granddaughter, Melissa, has she been living in France too?'

'No. That's kind of a far-out story, actually. She was dead. I mean, everyone thought she'd been dead for years. Her and her mother died in a boating accident, only they never found Melissa's body. She was a little girl then, and everyone thought she was dead too, everyone except Jacob Lions. I guess he always believed she was missing, and from what I hear, he's spent a fortune all these years trying to find her. And then, just a few days ago, there was a rumor going around town that they'd found her.'

'How?' Peggy asked. 'How did they find her?'

The waitress shook her head. 'The detectives, I guess. I hear he had a whole force of private detectives looking for her. It's been fifteen years or so, I don't know exactly how long. I was just a kid myself, you know.'

'Yes, I see.' Peggy nodded. She could not suppress a feeling of triumph. The return of the missing granddaughter, and Allison's strange behavior. It was just too much of a coincidence.

'Look, I've got to get back to work, people are starting to come in . . . '

'Thanks for all the help. I'm Peggy, by the way, Peggy Conners.'

'My name's Sally. Excuse me.' She hurried to a table where a family group was waiting to order breakfast.

Peggy, who had done little more than pick at her food, found herself too excited now to think of eating. She collected her purse, paid the check, and left.

Outside, though, her triumph faded a little in the bright morning sunlight. What she had learned had furthered her suspicions, but she had no more in the way of evidence that she could present to the authorities. If she was going to change the Sheriff's mind and persuade him to help her, she needed something concrete, something he couldn't dismiss with a scowl. She stood indecisively beside her car, head down, pondering her dilemma.

When she looked up, she saw Allison.

Allison was in the Rolls, in the front passenger seat, and driving the car was not Waldo, but Jack Lions. They were headed south, out of town; as they went by, Allison was saying something to Jack, her head turned away from Peggy, so she didn't see her.

Without a moment's hesitation, Peggy was in her car with the Jaguar's engine roaring to life. She darted out into traffic, almost taking the fender off an approaching Buick — earning herself a honk of the horn and a few choice words from the angry driver, but she had no time to pause and apologize to him. She cut in and out of the morning traffic, in pursuit of the Rolls.

Just when she thought she had lost

them, she caught a glimpse of silver-gray ahead, and in a moment more she was in sight of the car. She slowed down, hanging back, keeping at least two cars between them, so that if Allison happened to glance back, she wouldn't spot the Jag.

She wasn't sure exactly what she meant to do. She had a vague idea that if she went with them as far as they were going, she might have an opportunity to talk to Allison alone.

Out of town, the Rolls gained speed. That didn't worry Peggy. Old and battered through her car was, she knew it was an easy match for the luxurious sedan ahead. Nor was she the least bit afraid of driving fast. She was a good driver, and she knew it.

Ahead of her, taillights flickered red. The Rolls slowed and pulled into a gas station. Peggy bit her lip anxiously. She couldn't just pull in behind them without being noticed and there was no place to pull off the road between here and there. The only thing she could do was to go on by and hope no one saw or recognized her.

She pulled alongside another car as

they passed the gas station. She didn't dare risk looking over to see if they had noticed her. Once past the station, she changed to the right lane, slowing down. A side road branched off the highway just ahead and she turned into it. She waited, engine idling, looking back the way she had come for the Rolls to appear.

The time dragged by. She glanced at her watch impatiently. Three minutes, four ... surely it shouldn't take any longer than that to fill a gas tank. Could they have seen her, and turned back to lose her? Should she start back, and risk passing them going the wrong way?

She waited another three minutes. By then it was obvious something had gone wrong. It took her a moment more to back onto the busy highway. Slamming the car into gear, she raced back the way she had just come.

There was no sign of them at the gas station, nor anywhere along the road. She reached the town limits and slowed down, angry and frustrated. They had managed to elude her while she waited stupidly for them to pass.

She already knew a ferry ran from the point to the mainland. It was possible they had left the highway and come back to that, but when she drove to the landing she saw the ferry on the lake in the distance, already on its way. There was no way she could find out if they were on it, and no point in further pursuit.

Despondently she went back to her motel. She still had no plans. She was here and she meant to stay until she had at least talked to Allison. To do that, however, it looked as if she would have to return to the island; and how was she to do that without just being thrown off again, perhaps bodily this time?

Tired and shaken, she fitted the key into the lock of her door and turned it. At first, stepping into the relative darkness of her room, she thought the maid was in the process of cleaning it. As she realized the truth, she gasped and stepped back in disbelief.

Someone had ransacked her room. Her case lay open on the floor, its contents strewn about. The drawers of the dresser and nightstand had been yanked out and tossed on the floor. Even the bed itself had been searched, the mattress lying askew and the bedclothes flung about.

The bathroom had been worked over too; her cold cream opened, her perfume bottle lying empty in the sink, its contents apparently spilled down the drain.

She stared wide-eyed at the disorder, and felt the sharp, primitive pangs of fear. Who could have done this, and why? What could they possibly have been looking for?

* * *

The manager of the motel was very apologetic. 'We've never had anything like this happen before,' he insisted. 'I don't understand it.'

The police — not the Sheriff this time, but the local police — had been called at once. Peggy volunteered none of her own suspicions on this occasion. Without some evidence, something concrete she could show, she felt this stern-looking officer would be no more likely to believe her story than the Sheriff had been.

At any rate, there was no tangible evidence that the Lions family had any connection to this. On the surface, this was a burglary, pure and simple. A check had revealed that several things were missing. She had left some cash in her traveling case and that was gone, along with her transistor radio and a portable television that belonged to the motel.

The missing articles, however, did not convince Peggy that this was a simple burglary. If someone from Lions Island had searched her room for whatever reason, they would want to cover their tracks. They would likely have taken those things to hide their real motive. But what *was* their motive?

'Why only one room?' the manager asked.

'Hard to say,' the policeman answered him. 'These things don't always make sense. Maybe something scared them off before they worked the other rooms, or they thought Miss Conners here looked more likely to have something of value. A lot of crimes today, it's just kids, poor scared kids. No telling what goes through their minds.'

The manager nodded. 'If you'd like another room . . . ' he said tentatively to Peggy.

'No, that won't be necessary, if you can just have this cleaned up.' Whoever had found her in this room would certainly be able to find her in another if they planned a second visit. There was little point in moving. Whoever had been here was determined to find whatever they were looking for.

Only, what *had* they been looking for? The question stayed in her mind when the policeman and the motel manager had finally left her alone, while she was refolding her clothes. Something to tie her to Allison? Perhaps some evidence of Allison's real identity?

For the first time, she realized that if the Lions family and Allison were engaged in something illegal — and she couldn't begin to think what it might be — then she was a genuine threat to them, because she was the one person, at least in this part of the state, who knew who Allison really was. It was possible she might have some way of proving it.

Was it possible Jack Lions and Allison, having seen her following them and eluded her, had come back here to search the room? Surely they hadn't known where she was staying, but it was a small town. By now, local people knew who she was, and it wouldn't have taken more than a few minutes for Jack Lions to ask the right questions of the right people, and find her.

It suddenly seemed to her that she was playing a dangerous game, with formidable opponents: people who were used to having their own way, people with enough money and power to back up their arrogance.

*   *   *

In the end, it was clear to her that there was only one thing she could do, must do. She must go back to Lions Island, without the Sheriff or the lake patrol. She must find Allison alone and talk to her.

After that, if Allison still insisted on staying, on doing whatever it was she had set out to do, then Peggy was willing to wash her hands of the entire business. But first, she must see Allison.

That meant another journey to Lions Island, another visit to the great stone lions that guarded the gate.

As if her intention had sent out some sort of signal, the Sheriff came to visit her. She was surprised to find him at her door, and a little wary too. His expression on seeing her was not exactly a friendly or an encouraging one.

'Miss Conners,' he greeted her brusquely, nodding. 'I see you're still around.'

'Yes,' was all she said. He waited for more, some explanation or maybe some excuse. When he saw that it wasn't forthcoming, he changed his hat from one hand to the other.

'How long were you planning on staying, miss?'

'I'm not sure, exactly. A day or two, perhaps. Why, Sheriff?'

'Miss Conners, there are laws against harassing people and making a pest of yourself at their expense. I'd hate to have to lock you up, just to get you off people's backs.'

'Is that a threat, Sheriff?' Their eyes met in challenge, but he was not so foolish as to let that statement stand.

'No, just a simple statement of fact. You start harassing those people and I will enforce the law.' Then, his tone softening a bit, he said, 'Look, miss, why don't you take my advice and go home and wait? Leave finding your sister up to the authorities.'

'The authorities? Like you, you mean? How much effort have you expended in trying to help me find my sister? You won't even listen to what I've tried to tell you. What kind of faith can you expect me to have in the *authorities?*' She invested the last word with much angry sarcasm.

He had the good grace to look embarrassed. Lamely, he said, 'We aren't talking about a runaway child, Miss Conners, we're talking about an adult. Wherever she is, whatever she's doing, it's really up to her.'

'Is it? I want to find that out for myself.'

'Well, you've been warned, that's all.' With that he slammed his cap angrily back on his head and left. His effrontery both angered and dismayed her. She felt even more isolated than before, more removed from any real help. She knew now that she could only act alone, and in the face of official disapproval.

At the dock she made arrangements for a boat later that evening. She had decided it would be easier to approach the island unnoticed if she went at night. She had no exact plans for what she would do once she arrived there. She would trust to luck that something would happen to show her the way.

Of course, there was the possibility that Allison was no longer on the island. When she had seen her this morning, she might have been on her way to a new hideaway, some place where there was no danger of discovery.

A new idea had occurred to her, however. She knew that on the mainland they drove a Rolls-Royce, but she knew too that the boat she had seen Waldo piloting was certainly not big enough to transport a car. That meant the car must be kept somewhere on the mainland, presumably somewhere near where their boat was kept. She suspected these were not people who cared to walk long distances if it was not necessary.

It was not hard to find. Old George, from whom she rented the boat, pointed out a side street leading away from the docks, where there were a number of garages. Number twelve, he informed her, belonged to the Lions.

'But I wouldn't go messing around there, if I was you,' he added.

'Oh, of course not, I was just curious,' she assured him, but he had no sooner turned his attention to a new customer than she had strolled in the direction he had indicated.

The door to number twelve was locked, but there was enough of an opening for her to see a glint of silver-gray within. The Rolls was back. That might or might not mean that Allison was back on the island. There was really only one way for her to know for sure.

6

Her one concern was that in the darkness she might have difficulty locating the island; but she set her course in what she knew to be the general direction, and as she left behind the lights of the town, she was soon able to distinguish the soft glow of lights on Lions Island. There were floodlights at the boat landing, and further inland the lights of the house cast their own gleam. They turned the smooth surface of the water to a hammered bronze.

She skirted the island, avoiding the brightly lit landing. Surely those gates could not be the only way through the wall. There must be another exit as well, for safety's sake, and perhaps another landing.

She circled nearly all the way around the island, cutting her engine back almost to an idle and staying well out from the beach. She was disappointed in not finding another dock, but on the northern side the beach looked sandy and smooth.

When she saw she was again coming around to the lighted area of the boathouse and the gates, she swung back and made her way to the sandy expanse on the far side of the island. She brought the boat in slowly, as quietly as possible, and beached it.

She had sighted a cluster of rocks, and she waded in to tie the boat up to these. She tied it carefully. The last thing she wanted was to be stranded here.

Once actually on the island, though, she stood indecisively. She was outside the wall and, as nearly as she had been able to judge, at the rear of the house and beyond some utilitarian-looking buildings that she took to be wine presses and the like.

Before her loomed the stone wall, high enough to completely block her view. She supposed a real trespasser would have been able to scale it, but it looked to her an impossible task.

She had brought a flashlight, and had dressed in jeans and sneakers, unsure of just what she might have to do to get inside. For now, though, it seemed most sensible just to walk. She clung to her idea that there must be another gate in the stone barricade that encircled the island. She set off, following the wall, trying to find a way in.

She was soon glad she had dressed sensibly. Much of her 'walk' was over difficult, rocky terrain. In places, the wall came right down to the water's edge, and she found herself wading in water that once or twice came up to her knees. She scraped her hands and legs, and got what she was sure would be an ugly bruise on one shin.

When finally the wall veered away from the water and rocks, they were replaced by clumps of thick bushes. Pushing through them, she kept her spirits up by contemplating exactly what she was going to say to Allison when she found her.

'*If* I find her,' she amended glumly.

Finally, just when she was about to give up all hope, she came around a curve in the wall and found herself almost directly in front of a little wooden door. And now, looking out toward the lake, she could see the remains of what had once been another landing. This at one time must have been the back entrance, although it looked as if it had been many years since it had been used.

She pushed against the old door, holding her breath. At first she thought it was locked. It didn't budge. But she pushed again and slowly, laboriously, it creaked inward on rusted hinges. The noise that it made sounded to her frightened ears like the scream of a banshee, and for a moment she stood frozen in place, listening to the pounding of her heart. Within, everything remained silent and still.

Finally, her skin tingling with excitement, she stepped through the opening.

She was at the edge of a vineyard. A stone walk, crumbling and overgrown with grass, led along the wall, presumably up to the rear of the house. Off to her right, in the distance, she could see the dark outlines of the winery and the house itself.

Now that she was actually inside the wall, she was faced with the real question, the one she had avoided trying to answer in advance — how was she to find Allison?

'The last time, Allison found me,' she thought. 'She was out strolling. Maybe she will be again.'

She began to steal along the path, staying close to the old wall, as much out of the light as possible. Fortunately, the moon had not risen, and the house lights cast no more than a faint glow here.

She reached a huge, barnlike building, and crossed the path to pause in its shadows. Not far ahead, a rectangle of light spilled from a window, and she thought she saw a shadow flicker across it. Perhaps this was where a watchman lived, or even the chauffeur, Waldo. The building seemed to go on forever in the other direction. She would have to creep all the way around it, or manage to get past the lighted window unnoticed.

If only she had been able to see more of the island in the daylight, see beyond the walls and get the lay of the land. No doubt there were lawns and gardens about the house, and if Allison were out strolling, that would be the logical place to find her; but whether the lawns were in front of, or behind, or to the side of the house, she couldn't guess.

She took a deep breath and moved forward. When she got to the lighted window, she would simply have to crawl on her hands and knees past it, and hope that no one chose that moment to idly glance out.

Faintly, in the distance, she heard the sound of music. Someone was playing the piano, or perhaps it was a record. Chopin. The crisp notes seemed to drift and echo on the evening breeze along with the bittersweet scent of the grapevines. What an incongruous accompaniment it made it to the frightened beating of her heart as she sensed a vague danger, a presence . . .

And suddenly the music, the grape scent, everything, was gone; everything but her fear, and the feel of a pair of hands seizing her roughly, jerking her about.

Her heart thudding, she stared up into the angry, handsome face of Alex Lions.

'What are you doing here?' he demanded.

'I had to try to see her,' Peggy gasped

out, before her voice failed her. She stood quaking in his grip, staring wide-eyed at him.

When he suddenly released her, she was so weak-kneed she nearly sank to the ground. For support, she leaned back against the solid concrete of the building behind her. She knew she was trembling, knew he was aware of her fear. Perhaps that was why, when he spoke again, it was less ferociously.

'You are still sticking to that story?'

'Because it's the truth.' Somehow she managed to find the voice to insist on that.

For a moment, he looked angry again. Then, with a gesture that might have been impatience or frustration — she wasn't sure what — he grabbed her again, less gently than before, and steered her toward a door into the concrete building.

She was too disconcerted to resist, though for all she knew he might have been going to fling her down a well. Although she didn't think so. There was something about him; something not exactly kind, nor even pleasant, but something decent, a lack of malice.

He took her inside. It was dark and she could see nothing but a narrow beam of light that came from a slightly open door. He led her toward it.

Once inside, she could see nothing, the light blinding her after all her time in the darkness. Gradually, blinking and squinting, she saw that they were in an office; not a carpeted and paneled office like her father's, but a crude, working man's office, with a battered desk, the most ancient adding machine she had ever seen, and papers and books piled everywhere. It was cluttered and dusty, but it looked used and functional.

She saw too, now that she could look at him less fraughtly, that Alex Lions did not appear the wealthy scion of the family but more like one of his own workmen. He wore faded and dirty jeans, an old shirt open to the waist, and thick-soled leather boots.

All of a sudden, she liked him for his lack of pretension. She realized he had been out here working, rather than lounging inside somewhere lazily sipping a brandy. At the same time, she saw he was used to working. The hands that had gripped her so powerfully were a working man's hands, calloused and hard-looking, right now even a little dirty. And his face, his neck, the chest she saw exposed by the open shirt, had the near-brown color that is only acquired in days, weeks, months, out in the sun — a farmer's skin. A grape-picker's skin.

He went to one of the chairs and began to toss papers and books from it onto the floor. When it was empty, he even yanked a handkerchief from his pocket and wiped it clean — for me, she thought, surprised at the absurdity of such a chivalrous action being extended to her dirty, ragged, and soggy person. When he banged the chair over in front of her, however, she sat meekly in it.

He had not yet spoken since the encounter outside, but now he studied her with a hard, critical gaze. His eyes moved from her face — she managed a watery smile which he seemed not to notice — down her body, and came back to her face. She wished she didn't look quite so bedraggled.

He took a pack of cigarettes from his pocket, offered her one, which she declined, and lit one for himself.

'Now,' he said, exhaling smoke, 'start at the beginning and tell me again, calmly this time, what this is all about.'

And that was just what she did. She began with Allison's bad temper because she hadn't had her way about a summer vacation, went on to their trip to Hunter's Point, to that oddly fortuitous meeting with Mrs. Denver — that was the only point at which he interrupted her.

'Mrs. Denver — that was her name?'

'Yes. Do you know her?'

'There's no one around here by that name.'

She felt bold enough to push the question. 'But you know someone who fits the description. There is someone here on this island like that, isn't there?'

'There's a Mrs. Marvel lives here.'

'Who is she?'

'She is my father's . . . ' He hesitated, as if he found it distasteful to admit. 'His astrological advisor.'

She jumped up from her chair. 'Oh, she

must be the same, don't you see? Mrs. Denver knew everything about astrology. I know they must be the same person.'

She continued, speaking more confidently now. She sensed that his attitude had changed; not that he exactly believed her, not yet, but that he was no longer adamant in his disbelief. And he was listening quietly, carefully, to everything she had to say.

'And you believe the young woman you met down by the gates is your sister?' he asked when she had finished.

'I don't merely believe it, I know it. I've known Allison all my life. I couldn't be mistaken.'

He ran one hand through his hair, ruffling it even more than before. 'And I know she is Melissa Lions. Gilbert, actually, that was her father's name. She's my sister's daughter.'

'But how can you be so sure, if she's been missing all these years — ' He shot her a surprised glance and she added hastily, 'I've talked to people about town, about the family. I found out that Melissa has been gone since she was a little girl;

you couldn't have seen her in all that time, or talked to her. How can you know she is Melissa?'

He made an exasperated gesture. 'Do you think we are total fools out here on this island?' he demanded impatiently. 'You think if someone came strolling into the house and said, 'I am Melissa, your long-lost niece, and incidentally heiress to the Lions fortune,' I would just have accepted that blindly? I've talked to her at length. I've questioned her like a prosecuting attorney. She knows too much — things that only Melissa could possibly know, not things she could've gotten out of newspapers, or even with any amount of ferreting out. Things no one but Melissa could know.'

'She could have been coached,' Peggy suggested. 'Allison is very bright, she has a wonderful memory. Mrs. Denver, or Mrs. Marvel, whichever, could have told her all those details . . . '

'Mrs. Marvel didn't live here then. At that time no one here had ever heard of her.'

She said, less hopefully, 'Waldo?'

He shook his head. 'Not here either. Tell me, where did you say you lived, you and your sister?'

'Columbus.'

'According to Mrs. Marvel, Melissa was found in the girls' school in Connecticut. I've questioned her about that area too, and she knows it, too well to have just been coached on that also.'

It was Peggy's turn to sound a trifle smug. 'Allison was going to a girls' school in Connecticut,' she said simply.

That got through to him finally. His eyebrows lifted slightly and he studied her, as if he thought she might be making that up, and then clearly decided she was not.

He lit another cigarette, not bothering to offer her one this time, and went to stand at the window; the lighted window she had seen outside. She realized now that he had done this before, come like this to stand looking out the window, puzzling over something, perhaps this same problem.

He seemed for a long time to have forgotten that she was there, and she did not remind him or try to intrude upon his thoughts. She waited, no longer at all afraid of him.

Finally, he said, 'My father is ill, very ill, he doesn't have long to live. I can't have you poking around here, climbing in windows and crawling under beds . . . '

She started to protest but he silenced her with a look. 'I'll give you a chance to prove your story,' he said. 'But not here, not like this. I'll bring Melissa to you. You can confront her yourself, say what you like. If she is your sister, and I'm not saying for a moment I accept that, it shouldn't be hard to get things straight between you.'

'When . . . ?'

'When I can,' he said, a bit curtly. 'I don't imagine Melissa will exactly be pleased. No, don't start looking stubborn again. I'll bring her to you, to your motel. Now, I think it's time you returned to town and left me to my work. I've got a great deal I want to do, and you've taken up far too much of my time.'

She did not object, nor press him further for a commitment. She sensed that he would do as he had promised, and she let him lead her from the building and back along the walk, the walk she had crept along so stealthily a short time before.

'I'd forgotten this old walkway was here,' he said when they got to the wooden door through the wall, still standing open.

'I'm glad you forgot it.'

Luckily her boat was still there. The tide had come in, and they had to splash through quite a bit of water to get to it. He came with her, although she insisted it was not necessary. Was he just trying to be helpful, or was it simply his intention to make sure she really left? Peggy couldn't say.

At last, soaked, she was back in the boat. He waited alongside, standing in water that came almost to his waist, until she had gotten the engine started.

'I'll cast off for you,' he said.

'Thank you. And thank you for, for listening, at least.'

He said nothing to that. Their eyes met once again, but in the darkness she could not read the expression in his. Then he turned and made his way laboriously through the water to the rocks where she had tied up the lines.

He cast them off for her and stood waiting, watching, as she began to move away. When she looked back, he was still there, gradually fading into the shadows. Finally she could not tell if he was there or not, or when he might have turned back to the house.

She felt less frightened, less desolate now. Certainly less alone. She could not yet consider Alex Lions an ally — indeed, he had told her plainly that he thought Allison was his missing niece — but she felt strangely confident that at least he would give her a fair hearing. He had listened dutifully to what she had to say, neither arguing nor dismissing. And he had promised to bring Allison to her, so that they could talk things out.

Strangely, though, as she headed the boat back towards town, it was not seeing Allison that she was looking forward to.

It was seeing Alex Lions.

7

It was late when she arrived back at the town's dock. Old George had already gone for the day, but she had anticipated this and had made arrangements accordingly. She tied up the boat, leaving the key under the seat as agreed, and covered it with the tarp from the back.

The streets were quiet. Although this was a resort area, it was a family resort, with few of the late-night crowds, and few more swinging places. At just eleven, the town exuded tranquility. The sidewalks, as Allison would have put it, were rolled up.

Peggy herself rather enjoyed that. She had none of the fears she might have experienced walking alone at night on the streets of most big cities. If the good people of the town were abed, so apparently were the bad people.

Thinking of bad people, she was immediately reminded that someone had ransacked her motel room. And Allison and the Lions family, or some part of the household, were certainly involved in something less than legitimate. Even this vacation community had its criminal element, and she would be wise to remember that — to not let down her guard, to keep her wits honed, if she was ever to solve this mystery.

Alex's comments earlier had made her realize for the first time that Allison was not just pretending that she was not herself, she was pretending to be a rich heiress, granddaughter to a wealthy old man who was ill, perhaps at death's door. Allison — who had always been spoiled and pampered, who had always felt she was not getting her fair share, who always wanted more — craved not just money but all the accoutrements of wealth.

It was true that, for all their years together, for all their vaunted closeness, she had never really known Allison at all. The girl she had called her sister, the one with whom she had shared all the adventures and thrills, pleasures and agonies, of growing up, was in fact a stranger to her.

Perhaps, she thought wryly, we are all strangers to one another; going through the motions, pretending to know, to understand, to communicate, while all the time we stand behind glass walls.

She had reached the motel. Its rows of windows were dark, the other guests already abed. Her heels echoed hollowly as she walked along the row of locked doors. At her own, she hesitated. Perhaps her strange thoughts, the events of the past few days, or just plain tiredness were playing havoc with her nerves, but suddenly she was afraid to go in. She sensed something, an alien presence. For a full moment she stood with her hand on the doorknob.

Steeling herself, she went in. It was dark and she could not remember where the light was. On the nightstand, surely. Or hadn't she left the light on?

As if to prove to herself she was not afraid, she resisted her impulse to leave the door open for light. She closed it, and the room went black, as black as a tomb.

She took a step toward the nightstand, and froze, recognizing the scent of tobacco smoke. She turned toward the two chairs that sat by the window, and saw a glow of red, the tip of someone's cigarette. Faintly, barely discernible, was the shadow of someone seated in the chair, framed against the pale light at the window

She found the light switch, the one by the door that she had forgotten. It clicked, and the lights, soft, unobtrusive, came on.

Mrs. Denver smiled, a trifle acidly, from the striped Danish chair, her cigarette frozen midway in its arc to her lips. Under the veil of her hat, she blinked once or twice, owlishly. She looked younger than Peggy remembered. Younger and more menacing.

'I made myself at home,' Mrs. Denver said. 'I knew you would want me to be comfortable while I waited.'

'In the dark?'

'This light is so — so unflattering. A young person never thinks of that, but a woman of my years . . . '

She puffed at her cigarette, aggressively, intently. At the same time her hard, shrewd eyes observed Peggy through the cloud of smoke forming about her head.

Peggy, whose room it was and who ought to have been in command of the situation, was disconcerted. She felt as if she were the intruder here, as if she were somehow in the wrong. Defensively, a bit shrilly, she asked, 'What do you want?'

'Why did you come here?'

The question caught Peggy off guard. She crossed the room self-consciously and dropped her purse and sweater on the bed.

'I came to find Allison, as you well know.' She was disturbed but also a little angry at being attacked like this.

'Your sister is not here.' The cigarette glowed, faded, glowed. The veiled woman smoked rapidly, tensely.

'That's a lie and you know it,' Peggy shot back. 'She is on Lions Island. I've seen her and talked to her. You must be mad, both of you, to think that I would see you, meet you, talk to you, and not know who you are; that I could be talked into believing she is not Allison, that you are not Mrs. Denver, whatever name you use. Of course, I suppose you never thought I

119

would find you here, did you?'

'That's true. I thought you were a bit weak. Not typical of a Leo, mind you, but even Leos generally don't like to go to a lot of trouble. I thought once you'd made your inquiries you'd go haughtily back to Cincinnati — '

'Columbus,' Peggy corrected her instinctively.

'And wait, which is exactly what you should have done. Nothing here is any of your business.'

'You involve my sister in some sort of stupid scheme, steal her away in the middle of the night, and expect me to regard it as none of my business?' Peggy was incredulous.

Mrs. Denver ground her cigarette in the ashtray. It lay smoldering beside numerous others. She had apparently waited some time for Peggy to return.

'Not your sister, your adopted sister. No blood relation at all, really. She couldn't be, because she is Melissa Gilbert, the child Jacob Lions lost years ago: the child I have been searching for, that I found for him, that only I could have found for him,

120

because I knew better than to use his silly detectives. I used the one infallible source of information — the stars.'

'And they guided you to my sister?'

'It might interest you to know that I did not steal her away. I presented her with the truth, with the facts, and she came freely, of her own will.'

'Like a thief in the night.'

'She knew you would never understand, that you would only be a hindrance — a nuisance, as she put it.'

Mrs. Denver took a cigarette case from her purse. Peggy was stung by her remarks, which she knew had been intended to sting, to throw her off-balance. And yet, she could imagine Allison saying just such things; and it hurt, after all her worrying, after all her care, all her efforts, it hurt to think that Allison might have described her as a nuisance. She was silent for a long moment.

'So you see,' Mrs. Denver concluded smugly, once again puffing earnestly on a cigarette, 'it really is none of your business.'

Peggy turned angrily away, knowing

that she was being manipulated by this shrewd, heartless woman. Suddenly she saw, in a flash of insight, how much more easily Allison must have been handled. Poor, foolish Allison, with all her grandiose dreams, with her greedy ambition, it was easy to play on her ego, on her self-centeredness. This woman must have seen all that at once. Allison would have been putty in her hands.

'I will accept that,' Peggy said firmly, 'when Allison tells me so herself.'

'You will never hear it from her because you will never have the opportunity to talk to her.'

In her anger, Peggy nearly blurted out, 'I have already arranged to talk to her,' but even as she opened her mouth to say this, she checked herself. Instinct told her that Mrs. Denver might stop at nothing to prevent such a meeting. This was a woman of strong mind and will, a dangerous woman. Allison would never be able to stand up to her.

'We shall see,' was all Peggy said.

Mrs. Denver seemed to sense her confidence. It was her turn to be angry.

Her cigarette joined the others in the ashtray.

'I am not asking you, I am telling you, give this up. Leave here. Go home. If Allison chooses to contact you in the future, she will do so, without any prodding or snooping from you. You have my word on that.'

'I don't like being told what to do,' Peggy said, speaking slowly and evenly. 'You say that I have no claim on Allison. I deny it is so and I will not say it is so until I have spoken personally, and alone, with Allison. But far less do you have a claim on me. I did not invite you here, I do not know how you got in — how did you, by the way?'

Mrs. Denver only smiled. It was an ugly smile that did nothing to relieve the tension in the room.

'Well, however you managed it, you can leave now,' Peggy said icily. 'And you can remember not to come back. I'm here to find Allison, to see Allison. What you do neither concerns me nor interests me. In fact, we have nothing further to say to one another.'

Mrs. Denver got up from the chair. For the first time Peggy realized what a big woman she was. She had seemed willowy, frail even, sitting as she habitually did with her shoulders slumped, leaning forward. Her movements with her hands were so graceful that, combined with the soft elegance of her gray hair and her expensive, flowing dresses, they created an impression of gentle femininity.

Now, as she stood, Peggy was struck by how tall she was. She was wiry, an imposing figure of a woman who had used great skill and taste to overcome a certain mannishness in appearance. Her femininity, her fragility, were illusions, deliberately created. At the moment the illusion shattered, and Mrs. Denver was revealed for what she was — powerful and dangerous.

'I will warn you once more to leave here. You are meddling in things you don't understand, things that are none of your business. You may get hurt, and you will have only yourself to blame.'

Mrs. Denver took several steps toward her. Instinctively, Peggy stepped away, until the edge of the bed bumped against the backs of her legs. She felt cornered, threatened.

'You can't come here and threaten me,' she said, annoyed to hear her voice so tremulous, 'the police — '

Mrs. Denver gave a harsh, sinister laugh. 'The police? Have you forgotten I am from Lions Island? No one here bothers us. They dare not.'

Peggy wanted to deny that, but without genuine conviction, the words died in her throat. The authorities here obviously were in awe of the Lions clan. She was not entirely certain how far they would go in opposing them.

She no longer felt safe in the room with this woman, in the middle of the night. 'Please leave,' she said. 'If you don't go at once, I'll go to the desk and tell them you broke in.'

Mrs. Denver smirked. 'The Lions family owns this motel.'

Peggy sank down on the edge of the bed, at a loss for words. Of course that could be a lie, told to undermine her failing confidence. But it might also be true. That would explain how her room had been ransacked and the ease with which Mrs. Denver had come in to wait for her.

For all she knew, the Lions family owned most of the town.

Mrs. Denver came to stand before her, so close that Peggy had to lean far back to look into the woman's face.

'For the last time, you are not wanted here. You are not even safe here. Do you understand that? I will tolerate no more interference from you. I have worked too many years, long and hard, to . . . to accomplish something. Now I am within reach of my goal. I will not have you, or anyone else, destroy everything I have worked for. You will be gone from here tomorrow, or you will answer for the consequences.'

For a fleeting moment Peggy actually thought Mrs. Denver meant to strike her. Then, abruptly, she turned and stalked across the room. The door opened and closed, and she was gone.

8

Peggy was awakened by the ringing of the phone. For a sleepy moment she forgot where she was and lay, half-asleep, half-awake, waiting for her mother to answer the phone. Suddenly she remembered and, sitting up in bed, reached for the phone on the nightstand. It was the desk clerk.

'We have your bill ready for you, Miss Conners,' he said.

'My bill? I'm afraid I don't understand.'

'But I thought . . . aren't you leaving this morning?'

'No. Where did you get that idea?' As if, she thought grimly, she didn't know.

'Why, I understood . . . ' He floundered. 'I see. Perhaps I'd better look into this further.'

'You do that,' she said drily.

So, Mrs. Denver hadn't been bluffing, the family did own this motel — and how much more of the town? She got wearily out of bed.

She was not really surprised when the clerk called back while she was brushing her teeth.

'I'm afraid there's been a mix-up,' he explained, speaking smoothly now — too smoothly, she thought. 'It was my understanding you were only here through last night.'

'No, my stay is indefinite.'

'Yes, of course. But I'm afraid I've already booked your room. A reservation made well in advance and confirmed. You do understand, don't you?'

'Yes, I certainly do. Have no fear, I shall be out by check-out time.'

* * *

She had half-expected to find that the entire town would be closed to her, but as it turned out she found a room at the second place she checked, a small hotel in the downtown area. It was old-fashioned, but clean and respectable-looking — and not the property of the Lions family.

128

'I'm Mrs. Roberts, my husband and I have owned the hotel for ten years now,' the woman who showed her to her room told her. 'Of course, it's not as fancy as the new motels, but our guests often come back again and again; they like the homey atmosphere, they tell us.'

'And I'm sure I will too,' Peggy assured her.

'How long will you be staying, Miss Conners?'

Peggy hesitated. 'Not too long, I hope. Let's say a week, is that all right?'

'That's not a problem. Fortunately we had a cancellation on a reservation. Sometimes during the summer we're booked solid. I'll put you down for a week, then.'

'Fine.' Surely, Peggy thought, in a week's time she could accomplish what she had to accomplish.

Once settled into her new room, she strolled back to her former motel. For one thing, she wanted to leave a forwarding address. In a sense she wanted Mrs. Denver to know she hadn't run away frightened. It was like throwing down a gauntlet.

Of course, she knew Mrs. Denver

would find her anyway. It was a small town, and with the family's influence locally, she would know soon anyway that Peggy was still here and where she was staying.

She did not intend to cower in her room like a frightened mouse.

She had another reason, too, for leaving her new address. Alex Lions had promised he would bring Allison to see her, and for whatever reason, she believed him. She wanted to make it as easy as possible for him to find her.

Having informed an obviously nervous desk clerk where she could be found, she strolled into the coffee shop and took a seat. She had a vague hope that she might learn something more from the waitress, Sally, but as the woman approached her table, Peggy saw that she wore a sullen expression.

'Good morning,' Peggy said, smiling brightly. Sally mumbled a greeting and slapped a menu down on the table.

Peggy ordered coffee and toast, and when it was brought, made an attempt at conversation. 'I didn't realize when we talked yesterday that the Lions family owns this motel,' she said.

'Look,' Sally said, 'I don't have time to stand and chatter with customers, I'm awfully busy.' With that, she hurried back toward the kitchen. Peggy glanced around. At the moment she was the only customer in the restaurant.

She finished her coffee quickly and prepared to leave. Sally did not reappear. When a family of four came in, a different waitress came to serve them.

The day dragged by slowly. Peggy strolled around town for a while but, afraid she might miss Alex and Allison, she returned to her hotel room with a paperback novel and settled in to wait. Lunchtime came; she had a sandwich and some milk sent up, and continued to wait.

It was two in the afternoon when the knock came at her door. Afraid that it might be Mrs. Denver, back for yet another confrontation, she opened the door a mere crack.

It was Allison.

She looked angry and petulant, the way she always looked when she had made up her mind to be as difficult as she could be about whatever it was you wanted. Peggy knew the look well. At least, though, it truly was Allison, and she was here, with Alex Lion waiting behind her.

'I'm glad you found me,' she said, opening the door wide.

'They told us at the motel you'd moved,' Alex said. Allison said nothing, only glanced disdainfully around the plain, simply-furnished room.

'I had no choice. I had a visit from your friend — ' She glanced meaningfully at Allison. ' — who made all kinds of threats and insinuations, and then had me tossed out, practically into the streets.'

'You mean you were asked to move?' Alex looked annoyed.

'That's putting it in the politest terms.'

'I'll look into it.'

Allison had gone to the window to glance out. Now she seated herself in the room's only chair and tossed a defiant look at Peggy.

'What's this all about, anyway?' she demanded. 'Alex practically dragged me in here; against my better judgment, if you want to know. This had better be good.'

'It will be,' Peggy promised her.

'Look,' Alex said, 'I promised you a chance to talk. Alone. I'll wait in the lobby.'

Peggy threw him a grateful look. He nodded and went out. When the door had closed softly but firmly behind him, Peggy turned back to her sister.

'Now, listen, Allison,' she began.

'I am not Allison.'

Peggy slammed her hand down hard on the top of the dresser, making Allison flinch. So, Peggy thought wryly, she's nervous, at least, and with good reason.

'Stop it,' she said aloud. 'I don't know what sort of game you're playing, although I think I could make a pretty good guess. But I'll have no more of this pretense, not with me. Maybe you can forget all the years together, everything my family has done for you, our friendship — but I can't, and I won't. Argue with me if you must, but do not insult my intelligence any further.'

'I don't know what you're talking

about.' Allison sprang from the chair and began to pace back and forth like a caged animal. Her hands, where they gripped her purse, were white with tension.

'Why did you come here? Why did you leave in the middle of the night without a word? Why are you pretending to be someone else?'

'I am not pretending,' Allison nearly screamed. 'I am not the person you're looking for. I am Melissa Gilbert. Why won't you just accept that? And leave. That's all I want of you, that's the only reason I agreed to come here today to see you, to ask you, to beg you, to leave. You don't know what you're getting into.'

'Do you?' Peggy asked softly.

'Yes.' But Allison's voice lacked conviction. 'Oh, don't look so, so condemning. You don't understand any of this.'

'Then make me understand. Explain it to me. I promise you I'll listen and make every attempt to understand, to see it from your point of view. Start at the beginning, with Mrs. Denver.'

For a moment she thought Allison was going to give in and tell her, but then she gave her head a shake. 'There isn't any Mrs. Denver. Look, can't you just leave it at that? Can't you just go away and leave me alone? Is that too much to ask of you?'

'Under the present circumstances, yes. Oh, Allison, darling sister, this is not the first time you've gotten some hare-brained scheme in your head and gone off half-cocked to get yourself into trouble. It's exactly like that business with the dollhouse when you were seven, remember? Father wouldn't buy it for you, so you took it out of the store, thinking once you had it at home he would have to agree it was yours, and it would just simply be so. Only — '

'This isn't like that time at all,' Allison cried. 'That was different. I was entitled to the dollhouse. He'd already given you a new bicycle and . . . Oh!'

She caught herself, but too late. Peggy smiled and came across the room to grip Allison's trembling hand.

'Yes, you're right, he had given me a bicycle, and in your mind that made everything different. Just as in your mind you've already found some sort of justification for what you're up to here. Now, suppose you sit down again and tell me all about it, Allison.'

9

Allison slumped into the chair, looking defeated and sullen. There was no longer any pretense, nor need of any. Between them, at least, the game was ended.

'You always think you're so damned smart,' Allison said bitterly. 'But just for the record, you don't know everything, Peggy Conners.'

'I'm aware of that.' Peggy seated herself on the bed. 'But I mean to learn the rest of it. Now, just how did all this get started, anyway? Where did you meet Mrs. Denver?'

'She isn't Mrs. Denver, she's Mrs. Marvel.'

'With so many names, it's difficult to know which is the correct one.'

'I met her at Hunter's Point, that night at dinner. She was sitting in the dining room when we came in. She told me later that she'd watched us until you left. Then she came over and asked if she could sit at our table. At first I resented the intrusion, but she began talking almost at once. It sounded so intriguing. Of course, she couldn't explain everything, just enough to get me interested. And she asked me to meet her the next day, to talk more fully.'

'And you got rid of me so you could meet her by the lake.'

'Yes.' Allison at least had the grace to look a bit embarrassed by her subterfuge. 'Oh, I hated lying to you, you know that, for heaven's sake, but she had insisted that our meeting must be utterly secret. And she'd talked about a big reward for me if things went right.

'So, yes, I met her, and she outlined her plans. She was looking for someone to impersonate Jacob Lions' long-lost grand-daughter. I was the right age, the right physical type, everything. And if I got away with it, there was to be a big bundle of money in it for me.'

'There's one thing I don't understand,' Peggy said. 'That evening, on the terrace, how did she pick you of all the women she might have approached?'

For the first time in their meeting Allison's face brightened. 'That's the really odd part of it, Peg. She said she was guided there, to that place, at that time. She said she knew that when the right person came along, she'd be given a sign. Then she saw us come in, and order, and we had a glass of wine — Lions wine, remember? We even picked up the bottle and talked about the label. She said she knew at once that it was her sign, and that it was one of us. And then, when you got up and left, leaving me alone at the table . . . well, you know the rest.'

'No,' Peggy said, 'not all of it. I don't know, for instance, why you ever agreed to such a crazy scheme. Surely you must have seen that what you were agreeing to was illegal?'

Allison tossed her head disdainfully. 'Illegal? What nonsense. It's illegal when Father finds ways of taking things off his income tax that he shouldn't take. It's illegal when you drive over the speed limit, which you do all the time. And when Mother is having trouble sleeping and she borrows one of Aunt Grace's sleeping pills, that's illegal too.'

'But those are harmless things, of no real significance. Allison, don't you see, you could go to prison for what you're trying to do?'

Allison jumped up and began pacing the floor again. 'No,' she said.

'No, what?'

She turned to face Peggy and the look on her face was triumphant. 'No, Peggy, I can't go to prison for impersonating Jacob Lions' granddaughter.'

'Don't be stupid. You're smarter than that. Of course you can, this involves a fortune, a very large one, and fraud, and — '

'No,' Allison said again, firmly, 'I can't. Because, you see, Peggy, I'm not impersonating Melissa Gilbert — '

'You've been living here under that name, you've gone to great lengths to convince the family members, even the Sheriff — '

'I am Melissa Gilbert.'

Peggy stopped short, staring. The silence grew long. From outside Peggy could hear the sound of mid-afternoon traffic. Someone strolled past outside, whistling a tune. A fly had taken advantage of the open window and was buzzing insistently around the room.

'Allison,' she said in a whisper.

'Not Allison. Melissa.' Allison looked very pleased with herself.

'Allison, I don't know what kind of game you're trying to play now, but I'm not buying it.'

Allison crossed the room to her. She was bursting with excitement, with enthusiasm. She had already forgotten that Peggy had tricked a confession from her. Suddenly she was the old Allison, sharing some exciting piece of mischief with her sister.

'Oh, Peggy, you've got a closed mind, don't be like that. Think about it, just think about the possibility. Look, Jacob Lions lost his daughter and granddaughter in a boating accident fourteen years ago, on this very lake. The granddaughter was five. And fourteen years ago you found me on your doorstep in Hunter's Point. Isn't that a bit much for a coincidence?'

'Hunter's Point just isn't that close to here,' Peggy said, hardly able to believe what she was hearing. 'A five-year-old child, you couldn't have gotten that far without someone, the police or somebody, seeing you and picking you up as a lost child.'

'But you don't know how far I had to go, maybe not far at all. The boat was lost, it was never found. My mother's body was found east of here — halfway to Hunter's Point. For all we know, I was lost, or even deliberately left, at Hunter's Point.'

It was Peggy's turn to stand and pace in the narrow confines of the room. This was certainly an aspect of the situation she had never, in her wildest imaginings, considered. Allison — Melissa?

'No, I don't believe it,' she said finally, turning to face her sister. 'You were five, that's old enough to remember things. And never in all these years have you had any recollection of here, of the island, of your family.'

'Amnesia. I couldn't remember anything, don't you see? Not this family or any other. Something must have happened to block my memory of things.'

'And now I suppose you remember it all?' Peggy said drily.

Allison missed the tone of her voice. Her eyes sparkled.

'Yes, truly, ever since I arrived here, things have been coming back to me, all sorts of things.'

'Such as?'

'Why, even before we got to the island, I knew what it would look like, and the house, too. And my grandfather, I would have recognized him anywhere, even if I'd passed him on the street.'

'Perhaps because Mrs. Denver's — excuse me, Mrs. Marvel's — description of him was so excellent?'

'Oh, I'll admit,' Allison said, not in the least daunted by Peggy's skepticism, 'at first it was just a sham, a stunt, a way to have some fun, to give our family a hard time after the rotten way everyone had treated me. And I had a chance, too, to make some money, so I could have a real summer vacation. But that was before, Peggy. Now it's not a trick or a scheme anymore. Peggy, I know, I am Melissa Gilbert.

'Where does Mrs. Marvel come into all this?'

'She's my grandfather's astrological adviser. He's very big on astrology. When I disappeared, you see, he spent a fortune on detectives, looking for me. As my body had never washed up, naturally . . . '

'Naturally,' Peggy agreed.

' . . . he never accepted that I was dead. And there were no heirs, you see. He'd disinherited Alex, and Jack was just a poor cousin, no one pays any real attention to him. And then Mrs. Marvel came along. Jack found her, and she's the world's greatest at reading the stars. And she predicted, from reading the stars, that I would reappear. And that's what kept the old man looking for me all these years.'

'And when Melissa did not reappear as the stars predicted, Mrs. Marvel had to manufacture a Melissa — you.'

'She set out to find me following what the stars told her to do,' Allison corrected her, looking annoyed. 'Oh, why won't you believe what is so obvious?'

'To you, maybe, certainly not to me. Allison, look at it this way: even if you *were* Melissa, and you'll never convince me of it, don't you see you're still in a very dangerous position? From what you've told me, Mrs. Marvel is not doing this to be kind or to help the old man. She's doing it for what she can get out of it, presumably money.

'Even if your identity as Melissa is established, do you think she'll allow you to inherit all that money she has worked and schemed for? Not on your life. Once it's your money instead of Jacob's, then she'll start scheming to get it from you. There's no telling what she might do.'

Allison laughed softly. 'There'll be no need. You see, we've already worked all that out. I'll get my reward, and it's a very generous one too, and she'll get the rest, and we'll go our own separate ways.'

'I can't believe this,' Peggy said, angered by Allison's continued stubbornness. 'You, involved in something as shoddy as this, bilking a sick old man . . .'

'I've made him happy. He hasn't got

long to live anyway.'

'And what if Mrs. Marvel decides it's too long to wait?'

The quick flash of guilt on Allison's face told Peggy that Allison had considered that possibility — and accepted it in her mind.

'There'd be no need for anything like that,' Allison said, but she was sullen again. 'I told you, he hasn't got long to live. A few weeks, maybe, according to the doctors.'

'And you believe that once he dies, Mrs. Marvel will give you your money — a sizable portion of the fortune she's schemed to get — and let you go your own way? You, the one person who knows what she's done; you, the one who could expose her as a fraud? I think not.'

Allison's anger, when it came, was tinged with something else. Fear, Peggy thought. Fear because she too had considered the same question, and was far less confident of her answers than she claimed to be.

'You just won't listen,' Allison cried. 'I've told you the truth, the way it really is, but you've got your mind made up otherwise. Well, I don't care, there's nothing you can do about any of this; and don't try, Peggy, just don't try.'

'I can go the authorities. I can tell them everything.'

Allison laughed. 'What good would that do? They didn't believe you before and they won't believe you now. And you're forgetting the most important point. I am Melissa Gilbert. So I'm not guilty of anything. There's no crime in coming home to my grandfather.'

'And to your inheritance.'

'Yes, that too. Why shouldn't I have it? It's mine, isn't it? You're just jealous because it isn't yours, because I've done all this on my own, without your help or the family's. Or your blessing. You've always liked to think of me as poor, pathetic Allison — Allison the unknown, the unwanted, the burden. And now that I've made up my mind to be myself, you can't stand it, you want me always dependent on you.'

Peggy was shocked at this admission of how Allison had regarded their relationship all these years. She had never suspected any resentment, any unhappiness. In her mind, Allison had always been accepted and treated as a full member of the family.

And yet, had they from time to time been patronizing? Had they looked upon her as a burden, as a chance to show how good, how generous they were? For a moment, Peggy was forced to look into her own heart, to examine her motives in an effort to weigh the possible truth of Allison's words, to discover how such bitterness had welled up in her, made her so reckless, so full of hate.

'Oh, don't look so shocked,' Allison said sharply.

'I . . . I never knew you felt this way.'

'Of course not, because I never told you. How could I? I was dependent, at the mercy of you or your parents, for everything: for a place to sleep, for the food I ate, for the clothes I wore. And there have been times — not always, not all the time, but often — I've hated you for it.'

She snatched up her purse from the bed. 'This is my big chance, my chance to be myself, to buy a life of my own, and I won't let you mess it up for me.'

With that she was gone, the door slamming behind her. The sound seemed to echo in the room. Peggy felt drained. She had seen an Allison she had never known existed.

Perhaps, she thought sadly, because I never tried to know.

She went to the window and stared out without really seeing anything. Melissa? Was it possible?

And now that the harsh words were over, now that she could, so to speak, take a step back and view the matter calmly, she had to admit that it was possible.

Just barely, perhaps, but it was possible.

10

Peggy couldn't help wondering what Allison had told Alex, but he did not come up or call, and although she felt disappointed, she had to remind herself that had not been part of the agreement. He had promised to give her a chance to talk to Allison and he had kept his promise.

When all was said and done, however, she was not sure what, if anything, she had accomplished. She had seen Allison, and had gotten her to admit who she was and what she was doing. But things now seemed even more complicated than before.

She was at a complete loss as to what she should do next. She knew what Allison wanted her to do, of course. And perhaps that would be the wisest course of action. Allison was not a child, not even a blood relation. Peggy's only interest here was in Allison the woman; and if Allison did not want her here, as she strongly did not, then maybe it was time to leave gracefully.

Certainly everybody involved would be happier. Mrs. Marvel, Alex, Jack, the Sheriff. She frowned as she thought of one person who hadn't been consulted, the one person involved in this whole business whom she had not yet met — Jacob Lions. Would he be better off, or happier?

It was probable that old Jacob was happier in his delusion than he would be if she unmasked Allison. At the moment he was knowing the pleasure of having the girl he thought to be his long-lost granddaughter returned to him. He was dying, which must make his happiness in finding her even more poignant. Would it really be a kindness on her part to take that happiness from him?

At length, confused by her ponderings, she went out to stroll about town. She found an antique shop, and picked up a charming old carved picture frame for her mother and an old brooch for herself. In another store she bought notepaper.

All the while the same thoughts kept churning around in her mind. In despair she went to a movie, but after sitting for two hours staring at the screen she realized she had no idea what was happening in front of her, and left.

By this time it was evening and she had a cocktail and dinner. Finally, deciding to put her insistent thoughts to rest, she returned to her hotel room. She stopped at the lobby to see if she had any messages.

'No, sorry Miss Conners,' the clerk informed her.

The day had been warm but a cool breeze was blowing now through her room. She went to stand at the window for a moment. As she did so, her gaze went down to the street below.

Her breath caught and she quickly moved back, out of the direct line of the window. That man, standing in the doorway across the street — could it be Waldo? But what could he be doing there, as if . . . as if he were spying on her?

She peered out again, more cautiously this time, but the doorway across the street was empty. The man who had been there, half-in, half-out of the shadows, had gone, whoever he had been. She looked up and down the street. Several people strolled by but there was no one she could say with certainty was the same man.

She glanced uneasily at the old fire escape that ran up the building — past her window. It would be easy for a strong, athletic man to reach the fire escape from the street, and have access to her room.

She was annoyed with herself at her fears. To prove to herself that she wasn't really frightened by that scenario, she left the window open a little when she climbed into bed.

She did not sleep easily that night, however. For a long while she tossed and turned and stared at the patterns of light on the ceiling. The town outside grew still as the night deepened, and finally the noise of people still moving about on their business faded to the hum of the occasional automobile passing by, and once or twice footsteps on the sidewalk below.

Yet at every strange noise she started, snapping herself back from the sleep into which she was trying to drift. Was that a sound at her door? Had those footsteps paused just below her window?

When at last she did sleep, it was to dream: not the pleasant, gentle dreams of childhood, but a shadow-haunted nightmare. She was running, running through a strange, eerie forest. The bushes tore at her skirt and it seemed as if the branches of the trees reached down to try to entangle her. She was in a fog, so thick she could hardly see where she was going, and at first she did not know whether she was running from or to something.

She tripped and fell, but she did not fall to the ground as she expected, she tumbled into an open shaft that yawned up suddenly before her. Down and down and down she fell, into a darkness that grew ever darker.

It weighed her down, seeming to crush her, and the air grew thinner and thinner and harder to pull into her lungs. She was suffocating in the heavy, smothering darkness. She fought to breathe and could not.

All at once she knew, with blinding

panic — this was no dream. She was awake, in her bed, and she was unable to breathe. She struggled, but something was over her, upon her, something covered her face.

A pillow! Someone was holding a pillow over her face, smothering her in her sleep. She hit out into the darkness above, striking and clawing, and struck a strong, hairy arm, a wrist. She tugged frantically at the hand holding the pillow, trying to pry it loose. Her lungs felt as if they were on fire and the darkness had begun to rock and sway with her. Searing flashes of light exploded within her head. The hands holding the pillow were too powerful for her, she could not dislodge them, and she knew that she was fast losing consciousness.

She kicked with her legs, bringing a pained grunt from her assailant, but hardly loosening his hold. Her fingers clawed at the bed, the pillows, the nightstand — and caught hold of an electrical cord.

She yanked hard. The lamp on the nightstand toppled and fell to the floor with a crash, taking an ashtray with it. She clutched the nightstand and pulled at it too, knocking it over with another loud crash.

The noise must have frightened her attacker. For a moment he hesitated and the pressure on her face lessened. Then, even through the smothering pillow, she could hear a knocking at her door.

'Are you all right in there?' someone called and then, knocking louder, 'Hello?'

Suddenly the pressure was gone. The pillow was still there, so it was a moment before she realized no one was holding it down anymore. She flung it away, greedily gulping air into her lungs. The room still swayed and tilted when she tried to sit up. She had a glimpse of someone disappearing out the window, but in the darkness, dazed as she was, she could be sure of nothing more than that it was a man.

The room gradually righted itself and she became aware of the continued, increasingly insistent knocking at the door. Still gasping for air, she clambered from the bed and staggered across the room, flicking on the overhead light before she flung the door open.

By this time a crowd of people had gathered outside, including the owner, Mrs. Roberts, and her husband. 'Is anything wrong?' Mrs. Roberts asked. 'Oh, what's happened?'

'I ... I had an attacker,' Peggy stammered, clutching her throat. 'He tried to smother me with the pillow.'

Her announcement caused shock and dismay, and people crowded into her room, pointing out to one another the broken lamp and the tipped-over night-stand.

'Looks like we got here just in the nick of time,' Mrs. Roberts said, eyeing the bed and the pillow with wide eyes.

Her husband had gone to the window to peer out. Several others followed him, as if they expected to see the intruder still waiting outside. Of course he was gone, Peggy thought, but would he be back?

'Did you get a look at him?' Mr. Roberts asked.

Peggy shook her head. 'No, it was dark, and I was too stunned.' She had her suspicions about who it had been but she did not speak them aloud. They were only suspicions after all, and just now she didn't want to stir up any more trouble.

'I'll call the police,' Mrs. Roberts said.

'No, that isn't necessary,' Peggy said quickly. The hotel owner looked surprised.

'There's no point in it, really,' Peggy said, 'he's gone and he surely won't come back. And I couldn't identify him anyway, so nothing would come of it.'

'Well . . . ' Mrs. Roberts, trying not to look relieved, glanced indecisively at her husband. Of course they would be glad to avoid any further disturbance. Calling in the police in the middle of the night would not do their reputation any good.

'Nothing like this has ever happened here before,' Mr. Roberts said, looking unsure of himself.

'And probably never will again,' Peggy said. 'I think he was a would-be burglar, and he must have thought I was waking up and would catch him in the act. I'm sure he just panicked. But the bottom line is, I'm all right now, really. If you would just make sure the window is locked, to be safe.'

He righted the lamp and nightstand, and hurried to lock the window while his wife shooed everyone else out of the room.

'You're sure you're all right now?' he asked, pausing on his way out. 'I can call a doctor for you if you like.'

'No, I feel fine now.' She was still a bit weak, but otherwise she felt unharmed.

At last they were gone, and she could sink wearily into the room's only chair and try to think calmly over what had happened.

Someone had tried to kill her. Or had they? Had they only tried to frighten her away, as Mrs. Marvel had attempted to do before with her threats?

She closed her eyes and at once remembered that awful, numbing pressure, that moment in which she had felt herself sinking into unconsciousness. If she hadn't toppled the lamp and the nightstand over, would he have stopped, content to scare her? Or would it have gone on and on, until . . . ? She shuddered at that thought.

★ ★ ★

She was grateful to see the sun pouring through the window and to realize that she had slept the rest of the night without any further incident. For a moment she even ignored the ringing of the telephone, but at length it penetrated her awareness. She reached sleepily for the receiver.

The sleepiness fled when she recognized Alex's voice. Strange, she had spoken really very little with him and yet the timbre of his voice was as immediately familiar as if she had known him for years.

'I wanted a chance to talk to you again,' he was saying. 'Are you free this evening?'

'Yes, of course.'

'Good. Maybe we could have dinner, then?' He said this impersonally, as if arranging a business meeting, nothing more. Still, she could not help a little flutter of excitement.

'That would be fine,' she said. 'Around seven? Great. See you then.'

11

Shortly before seven she came down to the lobby to meet him. She had dressed with special care, picking a robin's-egg-blue dress that was full and flowing and utterly feminine. When they'd met on the estate, she must have looked like a drowned rat, and she wanted to offset that impression. She wore no jewelry but the antique brooch she'd picked up the day before. The stones, sapphire lookalikes, picked up the shade of her eyes quite flatteringly, she thought.

She had hardly stepped into the lobby when he came in from the street. He glanced quickly around, his eyes lighting on her. For a moment she thought he looked both surprised and pleased by what he saw, but his face quickly went blank, and when he came over to greet her, his manner was briskly impersonal.

His car, parked at the curb in front, was a modest Chevrolet sedan — a far cry from the family Rolls-Royce. There was, in fact, very little about Alex Lions to indicate a wealthy background. His manners were impeccable, when he chose to display them, and he had that sort of inbred confidence that often came with being raised in money, but there was nothing showy about him. Even his clothes, though good and neat, were no more expensive than the average young man was likely to wear.

'There's a place just outside of town that I like,' he said, driving with deceptive ease through the heavy traffic. 'The food's good and we'll be able to talk freely.'

The restaurant was unpretentious and comfortable. Alex had apparently been there often enough to be known and they were immediately led to a booth in a back corner, very much to themselves.

He ordered cocktails — a dry martini for himself, a vermouth cassis for her — and for dinner the prime rib, medium rare.

'The house specialty,' he assured her. 'Don't worry, you'll like it.'

'I'm sure I shall.'

162

The waitress served their drinks and left.

'Now, then,' Alex said, when they were alone, 'tell me what happened.'

Peggy hesitated. She had been debating with herself whether to tell him about the pillow attack, and her suspicions that Mrs Marvel and Waldo were behind it. But *were* they? She had told the Roberts that her attacker must have been a burglar — and that was certainly possible. If she told Alex about the incident, he would probably go ballistic, and confront the pair when they got to the mansion. It would poison the atmosphere, and put them on their guard. It would make it impossible for her to learn the truth about Allison.

Alex frowned as she remained silent. 'Well?' he prompted. 'Your meeting with Melissa — I trust everything was resolved to your satisfaction?'

Peggy shook her head. 'I wish it were, but we seem to be at an impasse.'

'In other words, you still insist she is Allison.'

'Oh, she admitted that to me.' His

163

eyebrows went up. Allison, apparently, had not given him a full report of the conversation. 'The problem is, she still insists that she's Melissa as well.'

She told him briefly of their interview, how she had tricked Allison into admitting her identity, and of Allison's insistence that she was really the heiress who had disappeared so many years before.

'The worst of it is,' she said, 'that as much as I argue with her I can't help but admit the possibility that she could be right. It's far-fetched but it is nonetheless possible.'

'She certainly had me convinced she was the real thing,' Alex said thoughtfully, sipping his martini. 'There are so many things she knows, things no one but Melissa should have known.'

'The thing I don't know,' Peggy said, 'is exactly what does she stand to gain? Oh, I know, she inherits some money, but just how much money?'

'All of it. The entire Lions fortune. As soon as Father was convinced who she was, she was in line for everything.'

164

Peggy was surprised and showed it. She had never dreamed how ambitious their scheme was. 'Then you of all people should be interested in discrediting her, I should think. Doesn't that mean she's going to get your share too?'

'I have no share, not in the Lions estate,' he said drily. 'I was disinherited years ago.'

'Oh, I see.' She was embarrassed at having dragged such personal information from him, but he shrugged it off as if it were of no consequence.

'No need to be embarrassed about it, I'm not,' he said easily. 'I was engaged to a woman my father didn't consider suitable. He told me if I persisted in the engagement he would disinherit me, and when I persisted, he did as he threatened.'

'And the woman?'

He smiled ruefully. 'When she found out I was no longer heir to the Lions fortune, she disinherited me too.'

'I'm sorry.'

'Don't be.' He sounded quite unconcerned. 'It was years ago and I was young and foolish. But I had too much pride to

165

accept my father's sympathy when it happened. I told him I had no desire for him to change his will again. All I asked was to be given the French vineyards to manage — they were new for us then — and to be treated like any other employee, allowed to make my own way. He agreed and I went abroad. I've lived there most of the time since, except for a few visits home.'

Which, Peggy thought, explained a great deal; such as why he looked like a workman and not a wealthy scion, and why he lived in such a mundane fashion, without the expensive clothes and fabulous cars she had expected of him.

'Was this before Melissa's disappearance?'

'Yes. I came home then, of course, for a time, but there simply wasn't much I could do, and the French vineyards needed me badly just then, so I went back.'

'What exactly happened, anyway? I know there was an accident, a boating accident.'

He shrugged and said, 'That's about as

much as I can tell you. When I went to France, my sister, Claire, was widowed and living at the house with her daughter, Melissa. Claire was very independent, headstrong, but she was devoted to our father, and she helped a great deal with the business. Apparently, though, they had a quarrel, and Claire decided she would go out in the boat to cool off. There was a storm coming up but that didn't discourage Claire, or even prevent her from taking little Melissa along.

'They went out, and never came back. They found the boat eventually, and after a time, Claire's body. That was when I came back. But they never found Melissa. I always believed she had drowned too. It seemed so unlikely that she could have made it to shore when Claire hadn't.'

'But your father always believed she was alive.'

'Yes.' He frowned thoughtfully. 'But that was Mrs. Marvel's doing.'

They were interrupted by the arrival of the waitress with their dinners and for a few minutes their attention was diverted from the subject of Melissa. The food was as good as Alex had promised and Peggy was surprised to find she was quite hungry.

'Mrs. Marvel arrived after Melissa's disappearance, is that right?' she asked finally.

'Yes. I wasn't here then either. I don't even know exactly when she did come. I just remember a reference to her in one of my father's letters. His new advisor, he called her. It was a long while before I knew that she was his personal astrologer.'

'Were you shocked?'

'Not particularly. Father had always been keen on things of that sort. I'll admit I was a little surprised to learn he'd hired his own personal stargazer, that seemed a bit far out, but at the time I didn't think it could do much harm.'

'But it did, you mean?'

'Unfortunately, yes.'

'You mean about Melissa, convincing him Melissa might be alive?'

'That was part of it. And it was stated not as a possibility, but as a fact. Apparently that was her introductory card: she came to him with the news that she had learned from the stars that Melissa was alive and would come back to him.'

'But the stars didn't say exactly when.'

He nodded. 'That's right. But he was so pleased by her news that he accepted it, and everything else she said. She started advising him in other things, every detail of his personal life — and eventually business matters as well.'

'And that's the other unfortunate part,' Peggy prompted him.

'Yes. I had no idea things were going downhill the way they were. I suppose Father's judgment starting going bad as his health deteriorated. Anyway, I gradually began picking up on some of the errors, even from where I was. And since I've been back, I've been discovering how bad, and how widespread, they really are. I'd have come back sooner, only I didn't know he was as sick as he is. He never mentioned it and nobody else troubled to tell me. All the people who were here when I was around, who might have gotten in touch with me, were gone.

Everyone on the island now has been hired since Mrs. Marvel came. Presumably on her advice.'

'I see. This beef is delicious, by the way.'

'I'm glad you're enjoying it. Would you like some coffee?'

He ordered coffees and sat back in the booth, more relaxed than she had yet seen him. Peggy finished the last morsel of baked potato and smiled her approval at him.

When the coffee came and their plates were cleared, she went back to their conversation. 'What about Jack? Where does he fit into the scheme of things?'

Alex seemed to regard Jack as of little importance. 'Oh, Jack's always been the family black sheep. He's only vaguely connected, anyway. A stepsister of Father's, her illegitimate child, that sort of thing. Anyway, he came around years ago, and Father took him in. But Jack's always been a bit of a recluse. He has his own apartment in the house, keeps mostly to himself. I don't suppose I've talked to him, really talked to him, more than half a dozen times in the years I've known him. For the rest it's been hello and goodbye in passing.'

'Might he be involved in Mrs. Marvel's schemes?'

'He could be. I don't suppose he stands to get much any other way. But it seems unlikely. He's such a namby-pamby.'

She remembered her meeting with Jack Lions. He hadn't seemed such a namby-pamby then. But Alex had not been around at the time. She could well understand that around his cousin, who was forceful, dynamic, confident, Jack might fade a bit, might step back into the shadows and out of the spotlight. But away from Alex, free to exercise his own sort of control — no, she did not think Jack Lions was necessarily so insignificant.

'There's one thing I can't help wondering about,' she said aloud. 'If you were disinherited, what would have happened to all the money had Melissa not shown up?

'I wasn't sure of that myself until I finally got it out of Father. It seems that, despite all Mrs. Marvel's advice to the contrary, he had finally given up hope of finding Melissa. He had decided to make a new will, leaving a modest settlement for me, for Jack, and for Mrs. Marvel. By far the largest sum would go to a research foundation he'd been connected with.'

'And that was the catalyst to set Mrs. Marvel off,' Peggy said. 'If she allowed him to go through with that, she'd get a few crumbs, but if she found Melissa, particularly a Melissa under her control, she stood to gain a fortune.'

'Interesting situation, isn't it?' He signaled for the check. 'It's getting late. We'd better get along. We have important things to do.'

'We? Important things?' She could not conceal her surprise.

'Well, I'll tell you the truth,' he said, counting out money, 'at this point in time I'm completely confused as to what the real situation is. I figure the only way I can learn whether Melissa is Melissa, or Allison is Allison, is to bring all the ingredients together, bring the pot to a boil, so to speak, and give it a good stir.'

'Which means what, exactly?'

He came around to help her out of the booth and she found herself being hurried along by his hand at her elbow.

'It means I know only one way of getting everyone involved together. You and I are going to Lions Island. After stopping at your hotel.'

'But why my hotel?

He paused just outside the restaurant. 'So you can pack, of course. If you're coming out to stay on the island, you won't need a hotel room too.'

★ ★ ★

It was the first time she had ever actually come up to the house, whose rooftop she had seen several times from a distance. How different it was this time to tie up at the landing with Alex and not have to be afraid of encountering him, or anyone else.

At the same time, she was sorry to see the boat ride end. When he had told her she was moving to the island, she had been too surprised to give much thought to the fact that she would be with him. There had been the quick trip back to town, the hurried packing while he waited in the lobby. Finally, they were in the boat, alone in the darkness, cutting through the water toward Lions Island — and suddenly she had become again aware of him as a man, close to her, drawn into the circle of his magnetic attraction. She had shivered, and he, seeing it, had thought she was cold from the night air.

'Come here,' he said.

She went to sit by him and to her surprise he put his arm around her. For a moment she sat stiffly, frightened by the intensity of her reaction. Then she melted against him and suddenly he was kissing her, and her heart was pounding.

All too soon, the world intruded. A wave made the boat tilt dizzily and his attention was brought back to it. It began to rain while he piloted the boat safely in to the landing. He kept his arm about her but he made no attempt to kiss her again, or verbally acknowledge the feelings that had sparked between them.

'Usually there's a cart here to drive up to the house,' he said apologetically, looking into the boathouse, 'but it looks like we'll have to hoof it tonight or wait down here till it stops raining.'

She had no objection to spending the time in the boathouse with him but she sensed that he was impatient to get to the house, to see his plan through to its conclusion. Now that she was actually here and partly free of the spell his kiss had cast over her, she had begun to feel a bit nervous. She had seen the glint of excitement in his eyes, and she had an uneasy suspicion that his passion in the boat had been in part an expression of his sense of excitement at the showdown to come.

'I don't mind the walk,' she said, 'and it's barely sprinkling now.'

The walk up to the house took no more than five minutes. For the first time Peggy was able to pass safely through the lions' gate. As she did so, she glanced up involuntarily at the stone beasts. They seemed to scowl down fiercely on her, no more welcoming nor less threatening than they had been before.

Beware, we stand at the gates of hell.
She shuddered.

'Cold again?' Alex asked, his arm again encircling her shoulders, but this time the warmth of his embrace did not dispel the chill within her.

* * *

The drive curved about a stand of trees and before them, suddenly it seemed, was the house, a massive Victorian mansion with fanciful turrets and gables, fairly drooping under the weight of its ornate gingerbread carving. A columned porch ran across the front and on either side was white latticework, open in a giant circle in the center. They entered the porch through one of the circular openings.

A thick, awkward woman in a maid's uniform came along the hall toward them as they entered the house. She stopped, surprised, when she saw Peggy.

'Good evening, Mrs. Brunner,' Alex greeted her. 'This is Miss Conners. She's come to spend a few days with us. Would you prepare a room for her?'

After a lengthy pause, during which Peggy half-expected her to refuse his request, she said, 'It's short notice.'

'Anything will do,' Peggy said quickly. 'I don't want to cause a lot of trouble.'

The resentful eyes watching her seemed to say, 'Then you shouldn't have come.' But the maid only nodded and went the other way, toward the stairs that led upward at the end of the hall.

'Waldo's wife,' Alex said in a whisper. Peggy nodded. That explained everything. She could hardly imagine most people being comfortable in a house with servants like those two. But then, Mrs. Marvel was not like other people, and Allison — well, Allison had her reasons for being content.

'If there's anyone about, they'll be in here,' Alex said, leading her to an archway that opened onto a vast parlor filled with heavy, dark furniture. At one end of the room a fire flickered in a huge fireplace, trying feebly to dispel the room's gloom. There was no one here, though.

'I think we could use a drink after that

rain,' he said. 'Brandy?'

'Sounds good.' She looked about the room. It was not a comfortable room, nor a comforting one. She supposed it had remained unchanged in appearance since the house had first been built. She could well understand that Alex would be happier living elsewhere.

'Don't worry,' he said, bringing her a snifter filled with brandy, 'it isn't all this bad.'

'It's pretty grim, isn't it?' she said, smiling.

They both froze as they heard footsteps in the hall, not Mrs. Brunner's heavy tread, but a lighter, more youthful step.

'Alex, Mrs. Brunner said . . . ' Allison came into the room and stopped, staring at them. She was wearing a white silk blouse and jodhpurs and looked very much the young aristocrat, the landed gentry.

How quickly she changed, Peggy thought, how easily she absorbed all this, as if she were indeed born to it.

'Hello, Allison,' she said tensely, trying to sound friendly.

'I thought we had all that out

yesterday,' Allison said in a frosty voice.

'Apparently not to everyone's satisfaction,' Alex said.

Allison turned on him as if Peggy were not even in the room. 'Why did you bring her here?' she demanded.

'Because I want to find out the truth, and it seemed like the best way to do that was to get everyone together in one time and place.'

Allison's angry gaze swept from one to the other. 'We'll see what Mrs. Marvel has to say about that.' She turned to leave.

'There's one thing you'd better be clear on,' Alex said in a voice that was all the more powerful for being so soft and low. 'Mrs. Marvel is no boss of mine. As far as I am concerned, she is only an employee of my father's, and not a very satisfactory one at that.'

Allison turned back at the archway to glower at him. 'More than an employee,' she said. 'She's a friend of mine. And there's one thing you'd better be clear on, Alex Lions: you count for nothing here. So long as my grandfather remains alive, you are his son and an employee, but

179

when he goes, you will be nothing more than an employee, and not a very satisfactory one either.'

With that she was gone. They heard her heels clicking rapidly along the hallway.

Peggy cast an apprehensive glance at Alex.

She could see he was infuriated by Allison's cruel reminder of his own tenuous position in the house. She sensed that beneath his usual composure he was a man of violent feelings. What would it be like if those passions were released, especially if they were directed toward her? He would be devouring in love, she was sure, and terrifying in hate.

'Welcome to Lions House,' he said drily, tilting his glass. She sipped more thoughtfully and made no answer, since none seemed to be called for. The chill of the room had increased despite the fire on the hearth.

Mrs. Brunner returned shortly. Peggy was almost glad to see her. Since Allison's brief and spiteful appearance, all the charm had fled from the evening. Alex had grown withdrawn and morose, and she could not guess what bitter thoughts occupied his mind as he stared into the fire, seemingly unaware of her presence.

'I have a room ready,' Mrs. Brunner announced. 'It is short notice, so you'll have to make allowances.'

'I'm sure it will be fine,' Peggy said. She had only the one bag, the rest of her things still back at the cottage at Hunter's Point, and Mrs. Brunner snatched that bag up as if afraid Peggy might have some other plans for it.

Alex responded curtly to Peggy's good-night and, with an increasing sense of apprehension, Peggy followed the house-keeper up the shadowy stairs at the end of the hall.

The house had electricity, but it had apparently been installed many years before, and sparingly. Only one dim light showed their way up the stairs. The room to which Mrs. Brunner led her was at the far end of the upper hall.

It was a small room but not much more cozy than the parlor below. The high ceiling was lost in shadows somewhere above. The bed was a massive four-poster, hung with heavy velvet draperies, and the other furniture — a bureau, a chest, an armoire — were equally dark and heavy. As below, a fire had been quickly started in the fireplace and now it bravely tried to hold back the encroaching shadows.

'Shall I unpack for you?' Mrs. Brunner asked coldly.

'That won't be necessary,' Peggy said. 'And thank you for your trouble. I know I was unexpected.'

'We do not often have guests. Good-night, miss.'

The door closed solidly after her. Peggy sighed and glanced around once more. She shuddered to think what nightmares a room like this might inspire.

The windows, two in one wall, over-looked the lawn and the distant vineyards. She was glad to see they opened onto a plain, sheer wall. No one could gain entry to her room from a balcony.

There was a lock on the door, too, and she threw it before she went exploring. The bathroom, an amusingly old-fashioned one, connected to a seemingly empty bedroom, its furniture still covered in dust sheets.

The white forms looked like so many waiting ghosts. The image brought back in force all her uneasiness.

It had seemed so much easier when Alex had proposed bringing her here. Now, alone in this dreadful room, all of her doubts and fears returned to assail her. She found herself remembering that the night before someone had broken into her hotel room and tried to smother her with a pillow. Chances were, that someone had come from this island, from this house. She had no illusions that Mrs. Marvel would take readily to her presence in the house. Allison certainly had not, and Jack, if he had any opinion at all, would undoubtedly side with Mrs. Marvel, since his fortunes seemed to be tied to hers. And the servants, as Alex had said, had all been employed by Mrs. Marvel and were likely to reflect her opinion.

That left only Alex, and for all his moments of tender passion he seemed to her as yet a very tentative ally. He had not yet indicated that he fully accepted her story regarding Allison, but was giving her a chance to prove it. If she could do so to his satisfaction she felt he would be strong, even tireless, in unraveling the threads of mystery that still surrounded Allison's presence here. If she failed to convince him . . . well, what then?

Of one thing she was sure. Everyone else in the house was determined to see that she failed. Everyone with one possible exception, the one whose presence dominated the house, the island, and yet whom she hadn't met, who remained perhaps the greatest enigma of all — Jacob Lions.

How would he react to her being here? Melissa had been a favorite of his, and for years the hope he would find her again had been the main influence on his life. Even if her 'return' proved to be nothing but a fraud, how would he react to such a harsh truth, old and sick as he was? He might well prefer to cling to his illusion.

She undressed slowly for bed, wondering if she had done the right thing to thrust herself into the jaws of the dilemma in this fashion. Jaws that at any moment might close fatally upon her.

12

Surprisingly, her first night in that gloomy old house, Peggy slept beautifully. The combination of the cool, fresh air, the distant sound of the water on the rocks, and the memory of Alex's kiss, overcame the fear inspired by the events of the previous night and by her less than friendly reception here.

She woke late to the golden sunshine spilling through her window, making the room seem less forbidding than it had the night before. Now it was just a funny old room, not entirely lacking in a kind of nostalgic charm.

By the time she had showered and dressed and come downstairs, Alex was gone — probably, she thought, out working in that disordered office. Mrs. Brunner, whom she met on the stairs, informed her that there was coffee in the dining room, and offered to prepare her breakfast.

'Just some toast will be fine,' Peggy

said. 'Is Alli- . . . Melissa around?'

'Miss Melissa generally sleeps late in the morning.'

Just like the old Allison, Peggy thought, but did not say. She did not ask about Mrs. Marvel. Hopefully she liked to sleep late also.

To her surprise it was Jack who waited in the dining room, giving the impression that he had been deliberately hanging around until she got up. He wore the seemingly omnipresent sunglasses and he looked paler than before, as if he had been ill. Or, she thought, very worried.

He greeted her in a friendly enough fashion, even managing a somewhat wry grin. 'You seem very fresh this morning,' he said, holding her chair for her. 'I surmise no one came into your room with an ax.'

She wondered if that were an oblique reference to the pillow incident in her hotel room. Did he know about that? Was he trying to test her, or even warn her subtly that there might be worse in store for her here?

'I slept like a log, thank you,' was all she said.

'The air here is very good,' he said, pouring coffee for her without asking. 'That's why I stay, although, at that, there has been a deterioration in air quality even here over the last few years. These days there's hardly anyplace one can go and feel safe.'

'And do you feel safe here?' she asked.

He smiled and said, 'Well, yes, from the standpoint of the air I breathe, at least. But as for whether it's safe for everyone, that's another matter.'

'Meaning, it might not be safe for me?'

'Sugar?' he asked, handing the bowl across to her. 'Of course, your situation here is quite different from mine. I live a quiet life, a withdrawn life. I keep very much to myself and rarely mix in anyone else's business.'

'And yet you've come to have breakfast with me.'

'I am like an insect, small, insignificant, fragile, even, but still I am drawn to the flower's beauty. When I heard that our table was to be graced by your presence, I could not bear to stay away.'

She laughed despite herself. The compliment was so old-fashioned, so

187

extravagant, that it was hard to take it seriously. There was a glow on his face, however, a lingering of his hand on her arm when he touched her, that made her suspect his interest in her might be genuine — at least, his physical interest.

'I can only say that if I've succeeded in prying you from a hermit's life, then I feel that I've done some good by coming,' she returned.

'Others may be sorry to see me.' He said this in such a self-deprecating way that she could not be sure if he was serious or not. 'I hardly fancy that Miss Melissa enjoys my company.'

A recollection flashed into her mind, of Jack and Melissa together in the Rolls-Royce, seemingly quite comfortable with one another's company. She very nearly mentioned this to him, and decided not to. Just now he seemed in a friendly, even a talkative mood, and it would be best to take advantage of it if she could.

'And what about you?' she asked, taking a sip of her coffee.

He grew suddenly wary. 'What do you mean?'

She smiled to put him at ease again. 'What do you think of Melissa?'

'Oh, you mean, do I believe she is Melissa?' He seemed to relax again. 'Why, there's no doubt of it. I knew her the moment she stepped into the room. Don't forget, I knew her as a child.'

'Yes, but that was long ago.' Peggy leaned across the table. 'A girl changes a great deal between five and nineteen. How can you be so sure?'

He seemed abnormally annoyed at her persistence. Maybe it was this intense nervousness that had made such a recluse of him.

'Good heavens, because I *am* sure,' he said petulantly, sounding almost woman-ish. 'There are things you just know. I was extremely fond of my cousin and her little girl. When Claire . . . when she was lost like that, well, I can't tell you what it did to me. I was shattered for weeks. I could hardly eat. I wonder that I even survived it myself. And like her grandfather, I never stopped believing that little Melissa would come back to us, it was the dream that kept us both alive. I would have known at once if this young woman were an imposter. No one could have deceived the kind of love that I kept in my heart for that little girl.'

Peggy was quite unmoved by this protestation. She was more inclined to think Jack Lions would be incapable of really loving anyone but himself. She had known men like him before, completely wrapped up in themselves.

'Of course, if it were to your advantage,' she needled him, curious to see what response it would provoke, 'it might be easier to be mistaken.'

To her surprise, he laughed. 'You are very stubborn, as well as very desirable.' He pushed back his chair and stood. 'But there is one thing you overlook, or perhaps you don't know. There is no advantage to me one way or the other. Whatever happens, my uncle has assured me that a small trust fund has been set aside for me, a modest allowance. Whether Melissa was ever found or not had no effect on those arrangements, and her return now cannot alter them either.'

'But if you cooperated with Mrs.

Marvel, if she had promised you something more . . . '

To her surprise, the smile left his face and his look turned dark and angry. 'Mrs. Marvel,' he said, almost spitting the name at her. 'I'll tell you this, and you can believe it or not as you wish. I hate Mrs. Marvel. I utterly despise her. She's ruined my life, she — '

'How has she ruined your life?' It was Alex, just coming in from the hall.

Jack flashed him an angry look and, without another word, dashed past Alex and out of the room. Staring after him, Peggy was still astonished by the intensity of feeling he had expressed. One thing was obvious to her; he had been telling the truth, at least about that. He hated Mrs. Marvel, hated her passionately. Could he, if he hated her like that, be in partnership with her?

'I do seem to have set him off,' Peggy said, smiling nervously.

'It's easy to do, I'm afraid,' Alex said. He helped himself to some coffee. Mrs. Brunner entered from the kitchen with toast and fresh rolls, and disappeared again wordlessly.

'But why does he hate Mrs. Marvel so? They've lived in this same house apparently for years. You would think if she was that difficult, he'd have gone long ago.'

'Except he has nowhere else to go and he's too spineless to just go out and fend for himself. But as to his hating her, that seems to be mutual. They avoid each other like the plague. He never comes down to a meal with the family unless he hears ahead of time that she's not going to be here. But they both refuse absolutely to discuss the matter.'

'How strange,' Peggy said, biting absentmindedly into one of the rolls.

'Now,' he said, looking and sounding like the Alex of the restaurant and the boat last night, 'I came in specifically to find you. I thought maybe for a while at least you'd like to put aside all this commotion and have a look around our little world.'

'It sounds lovely,' she said enthusiastically, her spirits lifting again. 'For once I can see it without skulking around in the dark.'

'I think you'll find it a great deal more

interesting this way.'

They went out through the rear of the house. In daylight she could see that in addition to the house there were three large buildings.

'The far one is where we press the grapes,' Alex explained. 'The smaller one is our bottling plant and also where we work on blends, and this last building is office and storage for the bottled wines. The ones we have to age or ferment in the bottles wait here as well.'

'Do all of your grapes come from the island?' From here she could look up at a hillside planted in vines.

'Good heavens, no. We have about three hundred acres along the lake shore, in three locations, and about a hundred acres in southern Ohio.'

'I didn't know there was a wine industry in southern Ohio.'

'That's really where it started,' he said, opening a gate that led into the vineyards. 'For years American settlers tried to grow European wine-grapes. The market for wine was always here. As far back as 1694, the state of South Carolina offered a reward to the man who could produce a good native wine, but the local vines, resistant to disease and already growing in profusion here, were overlooked in favor of European cuttings that inevitably succumbed to disease or the unfriendly climate.

'It wasn't until 1802 that a man named Major John Adlum discovered the Catawba grape growing wild in his garden and decided to try making some wine from it. Eventually he sent samples to Thomas Jefferson, who thought highly of it. But more important, he sent some to a man named Nicholas Longworth in Cincinnati. Longworth became the grandfather of Ohio winemaking. He planted his first vineyard in 1823, and in 1842, independently of French producers, he discovered champagne. Actually, he called it Sparkling Catawba. It was a great success. Longfellow wrote a poem about it and at one time there were complaints of French champagnes being relabeled and fraudulently passed off as authentic Sparkling Catawba.'

They were among the vines now. It was still early in the season and the grapes were no more than tiny clusters of green.

Here and there silent men passed along the rows, weeding and examining the plants — for disease, she supposed, or to check their growth.

'What happened to that early success?' she asked.

'Disease, mostly rot, wiped out the crops. Land values rose and killed other vineyards. The wine industry virtually disappeared in the southern part of the state, but fortunately by then it had been started here, in the north. My family was one of the first to plant vineyards here. The lake climate proved to be more favorable — the warm waters provided a longer growing season, for one thing. For years there was a flourishing industry. The Victory Hotel at Put-in-Bay was the world's largest at that time, and had the first swimming area where men and women swam together — very daring for its time. But Prohibition nearly killed the wine industry. Only a few survived. Fortunately, we were among them.'

He paused among the vines. 'These are Catawba grapes,' he said. 'They could be called Ohio's own wine grape. Over there,

195

past that marker, are Concords, and a few Niagaras and Ives. All native American grapes, and all becoming increasingly rare.'

'Are all American wines now made from the local grapes?'

Alex shook his head and sighed. 'No, it's pretty confusing, as a matter of fact. California wines are produced from European cuttings. They took to that soil and climate, as they didn't here. And eventually French hybrids were produced that adapted to this climate too. So, many Ohio and New York wineries now grow them instead of local grapes. And to further complicate things, France suffered an outbreak of mildew in the 1860s and imported native American cuttings, which were resistant to disease. They were grafted onto the French vines, so there's a little American blood in the European wines you drink.'

'Are things still bleak for the local wineries?'

'They're looking better. New acreage being planted, new wineries opening, especially the little, family-operated ones.

The Ohio wine industry is at a crossroads right now, and so is the Lions winery. I've had a great many fights with my father, trying to make him move more with the times.'

They had come to the building where the grapes were pressed. He led her inside, showing her the presses, including some antique ones.

'Lions is an old-fashioned house, noted for the high quality of its product. Everything here is done by hand. Whereas the larger winemakers ferment champagne in tanks, ours is still fermented in the bottle. Everything here is done by hand — the picking, the pressing. That maintains our reputation, but keeps prices up.'

'And you want to modernize.'

They went through to the next building, where the wine was bottled.

'To some extent, yes. I'd like to maintain a prestige line, hand-produced, and at the same time convert to modern techniques for the bulk of our wines, to produce a more competitive drink. Just as I finally persuaded my father that we could produce both wines made from the local grapes and new ones from the French hybrids. It took me five years to talk him into that — or this. This is one of my brain children.'

He lifted a bottle from a shelf and handed it to her. 'Our pure, natural line,' he explained. 'It contains no additives, no preservatives, and is fermented using only the yeasts which occur naturally on the fruit. It's risky, because of the greater chance of bad batches, but it's gone over well with the same customers who look for organically-grown foods.'

He handed her a bottle of champagne. 'Our finest product,' he said. 'Handmade, almost a lost art. By the time that bottle gets on this shelf, it's been handled over two hundred times. Eventually no one will be able to afford to produce wine that way. We lose money on every bottle we sell.'

'But why, at the high prices one pays in stores?'

'Taxes, for one thing. A gallon of table wine carries modest federal and state taxes, but champagne is taxed at a much higher rate, as a luxury item.'

'Pricing it out of the reach of the average consumer.'

'Exactly. Old-fashioned wines like this are only a labor of love. I'd like Lions to keep them, in modest quantities. But to survive, we'll have to go twentieth-century. Lions and the Ohio wine industry in general will eventually either find their place in the mainstream of American wines, or fall by the wayside.'

'What will happen to the Lions winery when your father passes on?'

He smiled. 'That, to be sure, will be a disappointment to Melissa. The winery can't be sold, and I can't be fired. When Father dies, I'm in sole control. The business and the money will belong to her, but I'll run the operation.'

Apparently Allison was unaware of that fact, judging from her remarks of the night before. And Peggy did not think she would be particularly pleased when she learned of it.

They spent a bit more time touring the facilities, and Peggy was persuaded to sample one or two of the family wines.

'Most of the wineries around here conduct tours, but we never have,' Alex explained. 'Father always felt that sort of thing got in the way of winemaking, at least for a small operation like ours, and in that I agree with him. Making fine wine is a work of art. A man can't do that and act as a tour guide too.'

It was nearly lunchtime when they came back into the house. For the morning Peggy had all but forgotten the troubles that had brought her here, but as they stepped into the gloomy main hall, she was reminded. Mrs. Brunner, hearing their voices, came into the hall to meet them.

'Your father is awake,' she said to Alex, ignoring Peggy. 'He's been asking about you.'

'I'll go to see him,' Alex said.

'No, not you,' Mrs. Brunner said, stopping him. 'He wants to see her.' She jerked her head in Peggy's direction.

13

She found she was trembling by the time she reached the door to the old man's room. Alex had come with her to show her the way. He put a comforting hand on her shoulder.

'I'll come in with you,' he said.

'No,' she said, screwing up her courage. 'That won't be necessary. After all, I don't want him to think I'm a coward.'

He gave her an encouraging smile. 'His bark is much worse than his bite, if that's any consolation.'

'Thanks.' She tapped lightly at the door and a gruff voice barked, 'Come in.'

She stepped into a cool, dark bedroom. She had a final glimpse of Alex's concerned face before she softly closed the door.

Jacob Lions was seated near the window, but the curtains were closed and the embracing wings of the throne-like chair shielded him from what little light there was, so that she had to walk to stand directly in front of him before she could really see what he looked like.

The lordly face that stared at her from the shadows increased her feeling of standing before a throne. He had the keen, penetrating eyes of a hawk. The nose dominated a hard, ruggedly-chiseled face that illness had not robbed of its strength. Even in youth this could not have been a handsome face, but certainly a compelling, intimidating one.

He wore a monkish robe that hid everything from view but his face and his hands, one resting on each arm of the chair. His hands, too, though veined and gnarled, had been powerful hands, the hands of a workman and not an effete aristocrat. Like Alex's hands, she could not help thinking, and this thought drew her to the old man even though his aloof, commanding attitude held her at a distance.

For a full minute he did not speak, but only continued to stare at her in a penetrating manner. At length, determined she would not be intimidated, she spoke first.

'Mrs. Brunner said you wanted to see me.'

He nodded but continued his silence for a few seconds more. Finally, he spoke, and his voice was the quavering ghost of the resonant instrument it must once have been.

'They tell me you claim to be Melissa's sister,' he said, fixing her with his wizened eyes. 'But you don't look like her at all.'

'Nor do you,' she could not help replying. 'In my case, however, it's simple to explain. Allison, the woman you call Melissa, is not my real sister. She's adopted. We . . . we found her when she was a little girl.'

'You found her when I lost her,' he said. He waited, expecting her to challenge that statement, but that was ground she had already covered with Allison, to no avail. She didn't believe that was what happened, but she could prove nothing.

At length, he asked, 'Why have you come here?'

'I came to find my sister, who disappeared mysteriously,' Peggy said. 'And I have stayed because I am afraid she is in trouble.'

The old man seemed agitated by that

answer. He moved as if he would rise from the chair, but his strength permitted him to do no more than brace his hands against the chair's arms.

'She is my granddaughter. She will inherit my wealth, the income from all this.' He traced a wide arc in the air. 'She has come home, where she belongs and where she is loved. You call this being in trouble?'

'She has always been loved and she has never been in want.' She saw a suspicious narrowing of his eyes at this and wondered what one earth Allison might have told him about her upbringing. No doubt she had made it as pathetic and dramatic as possible. 'I believe she has no right to be here. There's no proof that she is your granddaughter, and I think she is being duped.' She did not say it, but the implication was there, clear between them, that he was being duped as well.

'You are not afraid.'

She couldn't tell from his tone whether that was a statement or a question, and so she left it unanswered. He seemed to shrink further back in his chair, as if the interview had already exhausted him.

'I am old,' he said in a weary voice. 'I will not have time to search further for my granddaughter even if it were necessary.'

Was he actually admitting that she might be right, that Allison was very possibly a fraud? But when she opened her mouth to ask him, he raised a hand to silence her.

'I am tired now. Please go, Miss Conners. I extend the hospitality of my house to you, but I ask you to be a guest in it, not a source of further dissension. Now you will leave me. Ask Mrs. Brunner to come here, if you please.'

'Surely.' She went to the door but before she had reached it his voice stopped her again.

'My son, Alex, he speaks highly of you.' It was not a remark that required an answer and she gave him none. 'He is a fine boy,' he murmured. 'He has character.'

His chin sank down upon his chest. Whether he had fallen asleep or not she couldn't say. He made no further remarks and she went out. Alex had gone but Mrs. Brunner was just down the hall, obviously waiting.

'He asked to see you,' Peggy said. Mrs. Brunner hurried off to the old man's room. Left alone, Peggy made her way downstairs to the parlor, where she hoped to find Alex. Instead, she found herself face to face with Mrs. Marvel for the first time since she had arrived here.

The woman looked as eccentric as ever. She wore a knee-length smock over her dress and yet another wide-brimmed hat with a veil. She had evidently been working in a garden, as she wore gloves and held a trowel in one hand.

'So, here you are,' she said, smiling from behind her veil. 'Still trying to stir up your hornets' nest, I suppose.'

'Trying to get at the truth is how I would phrase it. The truth that you know as well as I do.'

'There are great many things I know that you do not. The stars tell me many things, my dear.'

'Just as they told you how to miraculously find Melissa?' Peggy could not entirely keep the sarcasm from her voice.

'The stars guided her to me and me to her. You scoff because you are ignorant, but the stars do not lie and they are never wrong. And that is why I know it was foolish for you to come here, foolish and dangerous. This way lies humiliation, defeat, even tragedy. You follow a willful star, dear girl, willful and dangerous.'

'And I suppose you will connive to make that prediction come true, just as in your predictions about Melissa.'

Mrs. Marvel took an angry step closer and for a moment Peggy thought she meant to strike her with the trowel in her hand.

'Young fool, leave here at once or you will have only yourself to blame for the consequences you will certainly suffer.' With that she whirled about and stalked from the room, leaving an ominous silence in her wake.

Alone, Peggy wondered where she would find Allison. Maybe another talk with her would do some good. And Alex had disappeared too.

When she went in to lunch a short time

later, she learned from Mrs. Brunner that Alex was working and had said he would not be back until evening. Allison was in her room. Presumably, Peggy thought, avoiding me — per Mrs. Marvel's instructions, no doubt.

Peggy spent a restless and unproductive afternoon alone. She strolled about the house and the grounds, hoping without much conviction that she might yet run into Allison. Once she saw Alex in the vineyards and he waved, but she saw that he was busy and she did not want to intrude. She even strolled down to the boathouse but Waldo was there, polishing the fittings on the cruiser, and the look he gave her was anything but welcoming.

Finally she settled in her room with a book from the library. So far, she reflected wryly, her coming here had accomplished nothing more than the stirring up of various personal animosities.

Still, that might not be a bad thing. Allison seemed frightened of Mrs. Marvel and resentful of Alex. Jack hated Mrs. Marvel and Alex had a not-very-flattering opinion of Jack. If those dislikes and resentments were brought into the open, even encouraged a little, who could tell what truths might surface?

Mrs. Brunner had informed her that dinner was at seven, and shortly before that time, Peggy came down to the parlor, wearing the only really good dress she had brought with her: a long, dark-blue velvet gown. This time both Mrs. Marvel and Allison were there, and soon after Peggy came down, Alex joined them.

Allison said, 'Well, here we all are, one big happy family.' She sipped a cocktail, and, at Alex's invitation, Peggy had one too.

'That's the closest you've come to admitting we're related,' Peggy said archly.

Having served drinks, Alex gave Allison a hard look. 'Peggy says that when the two of you had your talk the other day, you finally admitted to being her stepsister.'

'What of it?' Allison demanded. 'That isn't the real question, is it? The point is that I am Melissa Gilbert. Of course I lived a life in the intervening years since I was lost, but what difference does it make what that life was, now that I'm back?'

'Exactly,' Mrs. Marvel said. 'What can it matter if she was Allison Someone-or-other, or Mary Brown? She is now Melissa.'

'But is she?' Alex persisted.

'We've been all through that before,' Mrs. Marvel said impatiently.

'Yes, and I was convinced before, but now I'm just not so sure. All the things she knew, all the questions she answered — she could have been coached.'

'That's nonsense,' Allison said, putting her glass down on the table with such force that Peggy wondered the stem didn't snap. 'In the first place, there wouldn't have been time to coach me in everything I remember. From the moment I stepped onto this island I remembered everything about it, just as if I'd never been away.'

'There are many people who are familiar with the island,' Alex said. 'And with the family history. A good detective might have uncovered all the things you know, and a fast learner could have memorized much of it in a day or two.'

Mrs. Marvel made a scoffing sound but Allison only smiled confidently. To Peggy's surprise, she came close to Alex and put up one hand to toy playfully with the lapel of his jacket.

'And what detective do you think told me about the secret door in Grandfather's room, the door that leads to the basement, and from there, by a tunnel, to the wine buildings, and finally to the back gate itself? Do you think that is common knowledge too?'

Alex's face had grown pale. He took her hand from his jacket and stared at her in amazement.

'No one knew of that door or the tunnel,' he said. 'No one but Father and I.'

'So you thought.' Allison laughed softly. 'I discovered it as a little girl. Grandfather had the door open once when I came into his room and I made him show me the tunnel in return for my promise never to tell anyone.'

Mrs. Marvel had taken a step back and was staring at Allison with a surprise that equaled Alex's. She swayed slightly and put a hand to the mantel to steady herself.

Alex suddenly turned to her. 'Did you

know about the door and the tunnel?' he demanded.

Mrs. Marvel shook her head dazedly, as if she could not believe what she had heard. 'No, I never heard of them until now.' She turned slowly toward Allison. 'But then . . . if I didn't tell you about it, then . . . then you really are . . . '

She did not finish. Allison's gleeful laugh silenced them all for a moment.

'I've got to have some time to think,' Alex said. He went to the French doors that led to the terrace.

Peggy ran after him and grabbed hold of his sleeve. 'Alex, this must be some sort of trick, too. You don't believe it, do you?'

He stared down at her and for the moment she felt as if the two of them were once again opponents. 'I don't know just what I believe now,' he said slowly. With that he was gone. She stood staring anxiously at the door through which he had disappeared.

14

Alex did not return for dinner and Mrs. Marvel, seemingly stunned by Allison's revelation, decided she would have something sent up to her room.

'I feel faint all of a sudden,' she murmured, one hand at her breast.

Peggy and Allison went into the dining room alone. 'Now that there are just the two of us,' Peggy said when they were seated across from one another, 'tell me, how did you know about that secret door and the tunnel? And don't tell me you remembered it from your childhood.'

'Look,' Allison said, waving her fork like a weapon, 'if I'm not going to be allowed to at least eat my dinner in peace, I'm going to have something sent up to my room too.'

'Fair enough,' Peggy agreed. She did not care for having a meal spoiled either. In any case, she thought she could get a lot more out of Allison in a relaxed mood.

It was counterproductive to provoke her. 'Let's have a truce until after dinner.'

'That suits me fine,' Allison said in a sulky voice.

They ate more or less in silence, exchanging only a few desultory remarks on the dishes Mrs. Brunner served in her heavy-handed way. The food was good, solid German fare, heartier than Peggy was used to but quite acceptable.

Peggy's hopes for a more chatty Allison after dinner were dashed, however. Allison had no sooner finished her dessert than she pushed her chair back and announced that she thought she would retire early.

'I had hoped you and I would be able to talk a bit,' Peggy said, reproaching her gently.

'What for? We've both said everything we have to say already. Good night.'

Reluctantly, Peggy watched her go. She had begun to believe that nothing she could say or do would get through to Allison. Allison had set her course for a distant, and dangerous, star, and nothing now could change her direction.

Peggy went in search of Alex instead.

There was no sign of him in the parlor nor anywhere in the main downstairs room of the house. Thinking he might have gone to the office in the wine storage building, she left the house and followed the path in that direction.

That building was dark. She decided he must be in his room, or that he had left the estate. She walked in the direction of the boathouse, intending to see if all the boats were there. She had gone only a few feet when she heard footsteps behind her. She stopped and turned, expecting to see Alex, and found herself confronting Jack instead.

'I saw you from my window,' he said, pausing as though afraid she might bolt if he came too close. 'Since you were alone, I thought it would be a good time for a talk with you.'

'That makes you just about the only person on this island who wants to talk to me,' she said peevishly. She hadn't yet worked off the black mood that Allison's stubbornness had engendered.

'They're all fools,' Jack said flatly. 'Anyway, I'm the only one who might be able to help you.'

She was instantly alert. 'What do you mean, help me?'

He smiled mysteriously. 'Just that. I have something in my room that might make Melissa, or whoever she is, look like a fool.'

'What is it?'

He wagged his finger at her. 'Oh, no, you don't get anything out of me that easily. First, you have to come up to my room to see it. I refuse to bring it down here and I refuse to tell you about it.'

'You said, 'first' I had to come to your room. What's the second thing?'

He gave a low chuckle that sounded almost sinister in the moonlight. 'Maybe I'll insist that you give me a kiss,' he said.

She couldn't tell whether he was joking or not, but her determination to find some conclusive evidence against Allison's ruse was strong enough to withstand his none-too-subtle pass.

'Where is your room?'

'This way.' He took her arm, steering her toward the side door of the house.

She had thus far not ventured into this

part of the house. Alex had told her Jack had an apartment of his own, a suite of rooms on the third floor. They took the back stairs, past the kitchen. He paused at a door on the third floor.

'This is her room,' he said in a tense whisper.

'Allison's?'

'No, that woman's. Mrs. Marvel.' He seemed frightened at the very thought of her, and he held Peggy's arm in a vise-like grip as he hurried on with her to the next door. He had to unlock it with a large brass key he carried on a chain attached to his belt. Apparently Jack valued his privacy very highly.

'Welcome to my little world,' he said, ushering her in. She noted with some apprehension that he closed the door again behind them.

It was an apartment complete in itself. Through one open door she saw a small kitchenette and through another she had a glimpse of a bedroom. He could live here within the house and still not have to mingle with the others if he didn't wish to.

'It's very nice,' she said politely. Actually she thought it had an old-maidish quality she did not care for. She saw something else, too. A lady's silk stocking hung over the shower curtain rod in the bathroom. For all Jack's occasional prissiness, she apparently was not the first lady guest he'd had in his rooms of late. She wondered who. Surely not Allison?

'Would you like a drink?' he asked.

'I think not.' She did not feel the least bit comfortable with him in this remote suite of rooms. 'I'd rather see whatever it was you had to show me.'

Jack had a tense, excited air about him, as if he were about to spring a surprise. He went to a small bar and poured himself a glass of Scotch. 'Well, it's right in front of you, if you'd only use your eyes.' He added soda to his drink and stirred it with a silver spoon.

'I don't see ... Oh.' On her first cursory survey of the room she had given no more than a fleeting glance to the portrait that hung above a velvet settee. Now her eyes rested on it with surprise.

'That's her mother.' Jack came to stand just behind her. 'Melissa's mother, I mean. It's the only picture around the place. I got Uncle Jacob to give it to me years ago and by now I'm sure everyone's forgotten I have it.'

She was uncomfortably aware of his nearness behind her and instinctively she took a step forward.

'If anything could trip her up,' he went on, 'it would be this. She claims she remembers everything now that she's come back to the island — but if she didn't recognize her,' he pointed dramatically at the portrait, 'it would prove conclusively she's a fake. Surely she would recognize her own mother, wouldn't she?'

'Yes, I would think so,' Peggy said absentmindedly. She was studying the painting closely. Of course, part of its effect came from a trick of the light and the way the woman in the portrait wore her hair. And yet, on first sight, it had seemed to her . . . no, it was impossible. Still, the woman in the painting bore an unmistakable resemblance to Allison.

'How old was she when this was

painted?' she asked.

'Twenty, I believe. It was just before she was married.'

Almost Allison's age today. Was it possible after all that Allison was right? This was not an exact likeness, of course. One could probably find countless pairs of young women, quite unrelated, who looked as nearly alike as Allison and the long-dead Claire. But there was enough of a resemblance to support the actuality that they were mother and daughter.

'Has Allison seen this?' She wondered if Allison might have deliberately styled herself after the painting to further the illusion.

'Of course not. I told you, this is how we can trip her up.'

She couldn't share his enthusiasm. He had brought her here with the promise of something that would unmask Allison as a fraud. Instead, he might very well have provided further evidence to support her claims.

Jack moved close to her again and this time put his hands on her shoulders, turning her around to face him.

'Now, do I get my reward?' he asked. It was impossible to misread the desire written on his face. At the same moment, though, Peggy thought she saw something else in his eyes, some glint of mischief, as if he were hiding something from her, some private joke he'd made at her expense.

He leaned down to kiss her. 'Please don't,' she said, trying to twist free of his embrace. His face went ugly with anger. How mercurial his moods were.

'You promised,' he said, not letting her go.

'No, I didn't. Let me go, please.' She struggled with him. Suddenly he let her go, so unexpectedly that she nearly fell over the velvet settee. He was breathing hard and his voice was an angry rasp.

'You're just like all the others, aren't you?' he said.

'I don't know what you mean by that, nor why you should expect a woman to submit just because you feel inclined to kiss her. A woman is a person too, you know, with her own feelings and ideas, and rights.'

She strode to the door, half-fearing he would come after her or that the door would be locked. But he remained where he was and the door opened easily.

'Good night,' she said, glancing back, 'and thank you for showing me the portrait.'

He did not answer and she did not wait for him to pursue his amorous inclinations. She hurried down the back stairs. Above her she heard a door open and close. Jack? Coming after her? She hurried to the bottom of the stairs and across the empty kitchen.

Outside she paused in the moonlight, grateful for the cool night air. She wanted to forget the feel of Jack's fingers on her skin, the naked passion on his face as he moved his lips toward hers. She couldn't understand why he repulsed her so, why the thought of a kiss from him made her feel faintly ill.

She heard Alex's voice. She followed it, toward the side terrace. There was someone with him but the other voice was too low for her to identify. Then both voices stopped.

She came around the corner of the house and halted in her tracks, understanding in a glimpse why the voices had stopped so suddenly. The other voice had been Allison's, but neither of them noticed her at the moment. They were kissing.

Feeling heartsick, Peggy tried to turn away before they could discover her, but she was on gravel and the small crunching sound betrayed her.

'What was that?' Alex asked.

Peggy started to run, blindly, hardly knowing where she was going. Behind her she heard Alex cry, 'Peggy, wait!' But she continued to run. In the distance she heard Allison's laugh, cruel and taunting.

15

She ran blindly, with no idea where she was going, except to get away from them.

She found herself going in the direction of the boathouse. She passed through the iron gates and the stone lions. Did they look down upon her now with scorn and disdain, those cruel beasts that knew the answers to her questions, if only they would speak?

Beware, we stand at the gates of hell. Perhaps there was truth in that after all.

The small outboard motorboat was tied up at the dock. Hardly thinking what she was doing, she cast off and leaped inside. She yanked the starter rope and the motor leaped to life, and she reversed the boat away from the dock. Someone yelled her name. It sound unlike Alex's voice, but on the water it was sometimes difficult to tell.

She put the boat into forward and opened the throttle. The noise racketed the air as she gained speed. She really had no idea where she was going — not into town, certainly. What she needed most was to be alone, and she wanted the sensations of speed and wind and spray, and the covering darkness.

Already her mind was beginning to calm. She let up a bit on the throttle, steering out toward the open water. There were no other boats around. The tourists had returned to shore, to their hotels and motels. The fishermen were waiting for dawn. Overhead, she heard the whine of a jet winging swiftly on its way to some distant place.

Allison and Alex. Allison and Melissa. Melissa and Jack. Jack and Claire. Claire and old Jacob Lions. Like the paths in a maze, the relationships on Lions Island twisted around and around again. And in every path, standing in the shadows, manipulating, was Mrs. Marvel, always the evil alter ego.

Perhaps they had all been right, perhaps she should never have come. Perhaps she should leave now. She had confronted Allison and said what she had to say, and Allison had revealed a side of her nature that Peggy had never known existed, cruel instead of merely willful.

Right now Allison was living an illusion, but for all these years, Peggy had lived an illusion too, an impression she'd had of Allison that was only part of the truth, and not even the major part at that.

She heard the roar of a powerful engine in the distance. Another boat was out on the lake. She looked over her shoulder and saw a spotlight sweeping across the water. Someone was searching for something.

Searching for me? she wondered, with a sudden tingling of fear. She listened carefully. A big boat, bigger and far more powerful than this one. A cruiser, like the one in the boathouse at Lions Island. The spotlight swept over the water, left, then right, then left again.

'It's probably Alex, feeling guilty, wanting to apologize,' she told herself. At almost the same moment she flipped the switch, cutting off the running lights on the outboard. She cut back the throttle too, to lessen the noise of her boat, and listened. What if it wasn't Alex? What if it was another of those deadly threats she'd already encountered?

The other boat came closer, the powerful beam of light inching nearer and nearer. In a moment or two it would reveal her and her boat.

Gradually, hoping not to attract attention, she pushed the throttle forward and at the same time cut the wheel sharply to the right, toward the darkness that lay that side of the beam's sweep.

There was no way, however, to accelerate quietly in an outboard. The sound of her engine was like a shout in the night. The beam of light stepped in mid-sweep and arced back toward her.

Instinct took over. An inner voice told her that light was bringing no safety, no good intentions. It was like a threatening finger pointing at her in the darkness.

She thrust the throttle full forward. The boat hesitated for a few seconds, then surged ahead, nose lifting. The water was choppy this far out and her small boat bounced and slammed against the water, rocking and bucking.

She turned wide, hoping to throw off pursuit, but the cruiser behind her, its own engine now ascending in pitch as it accelerated, was too fast. Halfway through her turn the light caught her. She sat trapped in its blinding glare, her mouth open in a gasp of fright.

The boat bore full down upon her, its speed still increasing, the light holding her like a butterfly on a pin. They were going to ram her!

She grabbed the wheel and pulled hard to the right, flinging herself against the side of the boat. It veered, threatening to flip over, but it turned, seemingly into the path of the cruiser, but the turn carried her just to the side. The cruiser rushed past her, its wake flinging her about like a cork in a bucket.

She leaned forward against the dash, limp with fear. She was drenched and water stood ankle-high in the bottom of the outboard, but she was still afloat, and the cruiser, for all its power, wasn't maneuverable enough to spin around on a dime. It was slowing, turning to come back, but its turn was a wide, lazy-seeming one.

She pushed the throttle again and cried out in frustration. The motor had stalled.

Hands trembling, she pushed the starter button. The motor sputtered and coughed and finally died again.

She crawled to the stern, agonizingly aware of the water in the bottom of the boat, water that would slow her down, maybe even swamp her eventually. If this engine was like the one on their boat at home . . . it was. A little hatch lifted in the front of the motor housing, and there were the controls for the automatic choke. She flipped it off and crawled forward again.

This time the engine caught. She looked back and saw a giant eye of light staring through the night directly at her.

She opened it flat out, heading not for Lions Island but for where, if memory served her, the nearest inhabited island would be, somewhere off to her left. The boat shook and bucked beneath her. She prayed there were no obstructions in the water, no floating logs or other debris that she would miss without her running lights, debris that could send her boat hurtling into the air, end over end . . .

She looked back and realized with a

sinking sensation that she would never make it. Already the cruiser had cut the distance between them in half and it was gaining rapidly. The spotlight's beam trailed the water just a few feet behind her.

She no longer had any illusions that this was a friendly search for her. Whoever was piloting that cruiser intended to kill her. But who could it be? Waldo? Mrs. Marvel? Jack?

The obvious answer was Alex. It was he who had seen her, who had run after her calling her name. But why should he want to harm her? Had she trusted the wrong individual after all? Had his sweetness, his romancing, his kindness, only been another move on their part to throw her off the track?

The light caught her, hesitated, then struck her full in the back, casting her shadow eerily over the dashboard. Her boat seemed to vibrate in unison with the cruiser's motor. It looked like an awful monster behind her.

Again she pulled frantically on the wheel, to the left, then back to the right, cutting a zigzag course. The little boat was more agile than the cruiser. It was her only chance, the only possibility she had for escape.

The cruiser stayed with her, picking up speed. Incredibly, it still had power in reserve. This was a nightmarish cat and mouse game over the surface of the choppy water, and she was losing.

She knew she could never make that island now. Somewhere off to the right she saw the running lights of another boat. If she could get close enough so that they could see what was happening, surely whoever was in the cruiser would not kill her in front of eyewitnesses. And if her boat was swamped, there might be someone to rescue her from the water — if she was alive.

She swung hard to the right. For a second she lost them, the cruiser making a far wider and slower turn, but it was a turn that again brought them after her at an angle. She realized with a sinking in the bottom of her stomach that the angle would intersect her line of flight.

The light was on her left now, zooming down upon her like a demon from hell.

She tried to turn again, toward that distant boat that might mean rescue.

Once again, her engine stalled.

The cruiser roared past, slowing abruptly to turn back. Her legs barely supported her as she crawled back to the engine. She flipped the choke back and clambered frantically to the controls.

The engine wouldn't start. It sputtered and whined and refused to come to life. She heard the cruiser's engine slow as it made its turn and gradually begin to grow louder. They were coming back, again coming at a line that would strike her alongside, and they were coming fast, flat-out. The chase was over.

She cried in frustration, holding her finger glued to the starter button.

Nothing!

The light struck her full-face as she turned in terror. For a second or two more she hesitated. Then she leapt up, scrambling for a foothold on the vinyl seat — and dived into the water in front of the cruiser, directly in its path.

16

Impossible to tell how deep she had dived, how far she had swum. If she came up under the boat, or worse, into its propellers . . . She exhaled all the air from her lungs, diving deep, and swam with all the strength she had, down and forward at the same time, trying to swim under the length of the cruiser and come up behind it. Her lungs constricted in pain, they ached for air, and her limbs already felt weighted with iron.

Finally she could go no further. She had to breathe. She shot upward, searching for the surface. She broke it at last, coughing, choking on lake water and gasping for air. Her eyes opened on the blackness of the night, stars shining innocently above. Her arms still flailed at the black weight of the water and her legs kicked wildly. For a moment she was out of control and sank again. The cold water brought her back to her senses.

The lake, the cruiser in that horrible pursuit, the final crash even as she dived. She surfaced again, shaking the water from her eyes, and looked around.

She could see nothing of the outboard. It must have splintered at once from the impact. But there, further away than she would have expected, was the cruiser, not moving now, the engine down to an idle.

She trod water, grateful to feel a shoe slip from her foot. Her clothes were weighing her down and, treading water clumsily, she managed to get out of the dress and the other shoe. She looked again.

Darkness, and off there, to her left, some yards away, the cruiser, with its spotlight again sweeping the water, but just now in the opposite direction.

They would look for her, of course, whoever it was in the cruiser. They would want to make very sure they had been successful. The only thing she could really hope for was that they would give up eventually, conclude she was dead, and go back to the island.

The engine increased in sound and the cruiser began to move slowly, searching the water. Just now it was moving away at an angle, but she knew it would swing back this way any moment.

She began to swim. She wasn't sure how far it was to one of the islands or even how far she could swim. A mile, perhaps. She was a moderately good swimmer but what if she were swimming in the wrong direction? She might be swimming toward Canada, right out into the middle of that huge lake.

She lost track of the cruiser. Maybe they had cut their lights now, thinking to see her better by moonlight. The waves were just ample enough for her to get lost in their troughs. Her arms and legs ached and she had already begun to wonder if she could go much further. And still there was no sight of land.

Gasping for breath, she stopped to tread water, trying to rest a bit — and caught the scent of gasoline in the wind. A hundred yards or so away, she saw the running lights of a boat. The cruiser? She had no way of knowing, and she dared not shout for help lest she bring the wrong person.

She could hear the engine throbbing now, coming closer. And then the spotlight again, scanning the water, back and forth.

She dived down again, into that inky cold blackness, praying to heaven and to the ancient sea gods, to any ears that would listen.

When she came up, the boat had gone. She could no longer hear the muffled roar of its engine. A wave, perhaps a remnant of the cruiser's wake, lifted her and she saw trees in the distance. An island. She began to swim desperately in that direction.

Five minutes later, treading water to sight the island's trees again, she knew she would never reach it. Her arms were so leaden she could hardly lift them to stroke the water, and for all she could tell a shark might have bitten off her legs, as they were completely numb. She could barely keep herself afloat.

After another moment or two, she could not even do that. She was sinking into the water, carried down as on the wings of a sea god, some mythical creature of the deep, bearing her down to a place where the light was golden, and sweet music played, and the air was perfumed.

Much easier to close her eyes, give herself up to the dream that was enveloping her. Soon she would open her eyes again and it would be morning, and Alex would be there, calling her name . . .

He was there already. She heard his voice from afar. 'Peggy. Peggy.'

She was on the surface, some instinct keeping her limbs moving, and there was his voice again, calling, calling . . . but this was no dream, it was real, that was Alex's voice, and the boat was back, close now, and the light . . .

'Alex!' It was like a gasp, a murmur, carried away on the winds, over the lake, over the trees, far away to lands where men had never dwelt. 'Alex.'

Finally, she could do no more, would care no more, the dream was too insistent, too comforting. She closed her eyes and drifted into the waiting darkness.

★ ★ ★

She awakened to the pain of retching and coughing, and the realization that she was lying on the rough floor of a boat.

'Easy, there, easy, it's all right now,' a voice was saying. She opened her eyes and found herself looking up into Alex's concerned face.

'Alex, oh, Alex,' she tried to say, but what came out was a fresh burst of retching.

It was a long while before she was able to sit up. Alex took off his coat and wrapped it around her and bundled her into the seat beside him. Then he headed the boat for home.

'How . . . how did you find me?' she managed to ask finally, when the shivering had lessened a bit.

'I came after you right away but I didn't realize you had gone to the boathouse until I heard motors starting up. I came out in this one to look for you, and I saw all sorts of crazy goings-on with the lights, someone searching the water. I thought you were overboard, so I headed this way, but then the lights disappeared and the boat got away from me. What happened, anyway?'

'Someone chased me. They tried at first to swamp me. Then they rammed the outboard and I dived into the water. I was trying to swim to an island.'

'Who did it?' he asked in a low, icy voice.

She shook her head. 'I couldn't see. At first I thought . . . ' She checked herself, but not quickly enough.

'You thought it was me?' When she didn't answer, he said, 'My God, don't you know I could never harm you?'

They didn't talk after that until they reached Lions Island. Alex tied up the boat at the landing and helped her out. She felt weak but she was able to stand and walk.

He went straight to the boathouse. There was no doubt that the cruiser had been the boat chasing her. It wore the scars of the battle. The nose was gouged and splintered and one plank along the side had separated from another at the water line. It was still afloat, but whoever had been piloting it had given up the search for her not out of conviction that she was dead, but because he'd had to limp home with this boat before it too sank.

There was nothing, unfortunately, to tell them who had been piloting the cruiser.

He took her arm to steady her and together they walked toward the house. They saw no one on the way nor when they came into the house. It lay still about them, everyone seemingly abed for the night.

'Very cozy,' he said. 'Come on, you want some brandy to warm you up and a hot bath, then to bed. I'll straighten all this out in the morning.'

She gladly let him take charge. He poured the brandy, and while she sipped it in her bedroom, he filled a hot tub for her.

'Okay, in there,' he told her when it was ready, 'and then straight to bed. And lock your door tonight, as soon as I go out. Don't worry, I'm going to sleep just across the hall, in case.'

'Do you think someone might . . . ?'

'I don't know, but there's no point in

taking chances. And there's one other thing. I had no idea what I was letting you in for when I brought you out here, but now that I do know, I won't allow it to continue. In the morning, you're moving back to the mainland.'

She could not help a feeling of disappointment. She had come with such high hopes, but aside from antagonizing everyone and almost getting herself killed, she had accomplished nothing.

Just now, though, she hadn't the will to oppose his decision. She nodded mutely and went to soak in the tub.

17

Alex was waiting for her when she came down in the morning. Except for a slight cough and some soreness in her over-exercised muscles, she did not feel too bad from the night's misadventure.

She was regretting, however, Alex's decision that she must leave this morning. She felt confident now in his feelings for her, and so felt less threatened than she had before. With him as her champion, who would dare do her harm?

'Are you all right this morning?' he asked her first thing.

'Surprisingly, yes. Did you talk to the others?'

'Yes, but no one knows anything. According to their stories, everyone was in his or her own room, unaware anything was happening.'

'Well, there's one thing I know for sure. Someone was in that boat last night, someone who wanted me dead.'

'There's one other thing,' he said, looking down at his shoes. 'Last night, when you saw Allison and me . . . '

'That's really none of my business,' she said quickly.

'But it is. I want you to know. It was just, I was outside, looking for you, and she came out. She was teasing, I suppose, or trying to get close to me because she sensed I still wasn't sure about her. Or maybe she realized how I felt about you and was just jealous. I'm not excusing myself, you understand, it's just, it was so unexpected. I didn't expect anything like that, and for a moment I just stood there like an idiot and let her kiss me. And that's when you came along.'

'I understand,' Peggy said. Actually, she had heard very little after he said, 'How I felt about you.'

'I just wanted you to know how it was.' Then, very quickly, he closed the space between them and taking her in his arms, kissed her.

The kiss ended too soon, for after a dreamy moment she became aware that someone else had come into the room.

She looked over her shoulder. Allison had come into the dining room. At the moment, Peggy was glad to have Allison see them like this, to learn for herself that her childish prank of the night before was of no consequence.

The look on Allison's face, however, was something more than anger or jealousy. She looked horrified.

'Allison, what is it, what's wrong?' Peggy asked. She went to her sister and for once Allison welcomed the comfort of her embrace.

'It's Grandfather,' she said, sagging weakly against Peggy. 'He . . . he's dead.'

★　★　★

Jacob Lions had indeed passed on, succumbing to the years and the illness that had ravaged him so relentlessly. Peggy was saddened by his going, and saddened too that it put a wall of grief between her and Alex, just when they had resolved everything between them.

In a sense, however, she was glad Jacob had died with his illusions regarding

Melissa intact. He had believed to the end that his beloved granddaughter had come home to him.

The change in the situation brought home to Peggy more urgently than ever that Allison was now in grave danger from her fellow conspirators. Regardless of the way Allison had treated her of late, she could not just abandon her now.

She found Allison in her room. To her surprise, Allison seemed genuinely grieved by Jacob Lions' death. She was pale and drawn-looking, and smoking nervously. The ashtray by her bed was filled to overflowing.

'Allison,' Peggy said.

Allison turned red-rimmed eyes on her. 'How many times do I have to tell you the name is Melissa?'

'Allison, Melissa, that's not important now. What is important is that the old man's death changes everything for you. Surely you can see that.'

Allison smiled, a bittersweet smile. 'You're right, darling, it does change everything. It was one thing to go along with that old witch's schemes in order to get back here,

245

and while I was here to get myself squared away with Grandfather. But none of that matters anymore, as you say. He's gone now, and I am the heir.' Her face was positively triumphant. 'I own all this, Peggy. Not Mrs. Marvel, or Alex, or Jack, just me.'

'And you mean to tell them that? You mean to turn your back on Mrs. Marvel?'

'There's nothing she can do.' Allison blew another cloud of smoke into the already smoke-filled room. 'Once the will's probated, it'll be mine, completely mine. I intend to boot her out.'

Peggy sat on the edge of the bed and clasped one of Allison's hands in her own. 'And you think she'll take that lying down?'

Allison looked suddenly uncertain. 'I . . . I don't know.'

'I think you do know. I think it's important that you come away from here. Leave it to Alex or Jack or the authorities to get rid of Mrs. Marvel and Waldo. Don't you see, Mrs. Marvel has plotted all these years for this, she won't let you just snatch it all out of her hands. I don't know what she'll do, but my guess is that the minute she hears of your intentions, your life is going to be in grave danger.'

Allison puffed thoughtfully for a moment. 'You may be right,' she said finally.

'I know I am. Look, it doesn't matter what's happened between you and me. You don't even have to come home with me, just leave with me, and go somewhere, anywhere, until she's out of here and the will has been probated.'

At the moment Peggy did not even care whether Allison thought she believed her or not. Just now she was thinking only of Allison's safety.

For the first time since she had disappeared from Hunter's Point, Allison gave her a genuinely friendly smile. 'It's sweet of you to worry about me, really, Peg. I know I have been a pill of late. Look, don't worry, I'll tell you what, I'll come to your hotel tonight. I won't come back to Columbus with you, that part of my life is finished, but I'll leave with you tonight and we can go someplace, until I can get settled in.'

Peggy squeezed her hand affectionately. 'I'm glad you see it that way. And remember, don't say anything to Mrs. Marvel about what you've got planned.'

'Don't worry, she won't stop me.' It was not exactly the promise Peggy had wanted, but she did not want to risk Allison's newly friendly mood by pressing her for more.

'Till tonight, then.'

Allison flashed a smile that Peggy thought was a little too bright, a little too tense, but she smiled back and left the room.

She found Alex in the hall looking for her. His face was lined and weary, but he took her warmly in his arms.

'Look,' he said, 'I've got to go into town. There are the authorities to see, and Father's lawyers to contact, and business affairs that will have to be taken care of. And I don't want to leave you here on your own. How soon can you get your things together?'

'It'll only take me a few minutes,' Peggy said. Now that she had persuaded Allison to come away, she did not regret leaving

Lions Island, and Alex would be too busy over the next day or so to have time for her.

'Good, I'll meet you in the parlor,' he said.

When she came down to the parlor less than half an hour later, however, it was Jack, not Alex, who was sitting there. He rose and greeted her as warmly as if there had been no quarrel between them the night before.

'You're not leaving?' he exclaimed, seeing her suitcase.

'Yes. I think I'll be more comfortable in town.'

'But there's no need to dash away, just because Uncle Jacob passed on. He'd want you to stay, I'm sure. And you needn't worry about Mrs. Marvel, she's under the weather today. Too much night air, I suppose.'

His eyes held a malicious glint of amusement, as if he knew something secret and wicked. Was he hinting that Mrs. Marvel had been the one in the boat last night?

'What do you mean, too much night

air? Was she out on the lake last night?'

Jack shrugged and chuckled. 'She wouldn't like me to tell everything I know. Besides, you didn't reward me properly the last time I shared one of my secrets with you.'

He put a hand on her arm. Despite herself, she felt the same revulsion she had felt last night when he had tried to kiss her. She pulled her arm away.

'Do you know who tried to kill me last night?' she asked boldly.

'I know who tried to kiss you,' he replied with a maddening snicker.

'And I know who's going to lose his teeth if he tries it again,' Alex said from the doorway.

Jack, looking genuinely frightened, yanked his hand from Peggy's arm and back away from her. 'I was only being friendly,' he said in a whine. 'You should be grateful, I'm the only one who's tried to make her welcome here.'

He did not wait for a reply but hurried from the room. Peggy didn't know whether to be pleased by Alex's display of jealousy or annoyed that he might have interrupted an important bit of news. In any case, the damage was done.

'I'll just be a few minutes more,' Alex said. 'Sorry to keep you waiting but I've got a couple more phone calls to make.'

'I don't mind. I'll meet you down at the boat.'

When he had left her, however, her thoughts went back to Mrs. Marvel, and Jack's veiled hints. Could it have been Mrs. Marvel in the cruiser last night? The woman had an air of frailty about her but she was a big woman, and certainly strong enough to handle a boat like a man. Jack had said she was sick today. Maybe this would be a perfect time to visit her. It might be that, feeling under the weather, she would be less on her guard than before.

She went to the third floor and knocked on the door of Mrs. Marvel's room. There was a brief silence and then a strained voice asked, 'Who is it?'

'It's Peggy.'

'What do you want?' She sounded surprised.

'Jack said you were ill. I thought I'd

look in on you. May I come in?'

There was another silence, and then, 'Wait just a moment.'

Peggy waited in silence. There were sounds from inside that she couldn't identify, and the creak of a floorboard as someone crossed a room. When she was just beginning to think Mrs. Marvel wouldn't see her, the voice from within called, 'You can come in now.'

The room was nearly as dark as night. Only the light that spilled in from the hall and a faint glow from the thickly curtained windows made it possible for Peggy to make out the heavy furniture.

'What do you want?' Mrs. Marvel's familiar voice asked from the bed.

Peggy came closer, but even standing by the bed she was barely able to distinguish the woman sitting up in it.

'I just wanted to see how you were feeling. Would you like me to turn on a light?' Peggy reached for the switch but Mrs. Marvel stopped her with a quick, 'No, I have a headache. The light makes it worse.'

'Oh, I see, I'm sorry.'

Another long and awkward silence followed. Finally, Mrs. Marvel said, 'Mrs. Brunner tells me the old man is dead.'

'Yes.'

'I saw that in the stars as well. I knew his time had come. And yours has come too. There's nothing more to keep you here.'

'I'm going,' Peggy said. 'I'm leaving in a few minutes.'

She sensed that this time she had succeeded in surprising the woman in the bed. The springs creaked and the bedclothes rustled as she held them up to her chin.

'No one told me,' she said sharply.

'I saw no reason to make an announcement of it.'

'Well, I must say, I'm glad to hear it. You were foolish to come here in the first place, as I told you before. There was nothing you could do, then or now.'

'Perhaps.' There was another weighty silence. This time Mrs. Marvel did not break it and, feeling she was getting nowhere, Peggy decided to go.

'I just wanted to wish you well,' she said, turning toward the door. 'Goodbye.'

'You're leaving right away? Leaving the island, I mean?'

'Yes, in a few minutes.'

'Goodbye, then.'

As the door closed behind her, Peggy heard Mrs. Marvel clambering out of bed. Apparently her news had cured Mrs. Marvel's indisposition. She wondered who or what she was hurrying off to see — Allison? Waldo? Jack? As much as she and Jack hated one another, they were two of a kind, more alike than either of them would probably want to admit.

At least, she told herself, hurrying to the boat landing, I'm out of it all now, whatever happens.

18

Alex was in complete agreement with Peggy's efforts to get Allison out of the house. 'If she was in collusion with Mrs. Marvel, and plans now on ditching her, she'd be a fool to stay around and wait for Mrs. Marvel to leave,' he said. 'That woman is capable of just about anything.'

'Allison said she'd see me tonight. I don't know exactly what she'll agree to do, but if we leave town I'll let you know where we are.'

'Fine. I'll be pretty tied up the next day or two anyway. Just make sure you don't stay lost.'

'Small chance,' she said, laughing.

They parted at the town landing, with her insistence that there was no need for him to see her to the hotel. She watched him go until the boat had dwindled to a spot in the distance. Then she strolled nonchalantly back to the hotel. Mrs. Roberts had promised to save her room for her, and in no time Peggy was once again comfortably installed there.

After lunch, she put in a call to Columbus. She did not give her mother the full story of everything that had happened, but she assured her that Allison was all right. 'And it looks like she's to be an heiress,' she added.

'It all sounds very mysterious, is all I can say. How about you? Are you all right? You sound like you've gotten a cold.'

'I'm fine, really. I got a little wet last night,' Peggy said, smiling into the receiver. She saw no point in upsetting her parents by telling them what actually had happened. In any case, that was history now. With Jacob Lions dead and Allison preparing to leave the island, Peggy regarded her part in the drama as ended. She was certainly not in any more danger, as no one now had any reason to want to be rid of her.

She spent a lazy afternoon strolling about town, feeling more relaxed than she had been since she arrived there, and for the first time she could actually enjoy the resort town atmosphere. As evening approached she had an early dinner and went back to her room to wait for Allison.

Allison phoned her room shortly before eight. 'I'm in the lobby,' she said, sounding breathless and uncertain. 'I just wanted to be sure you were there before I came up.'

'No problems getting away?'

Allison paused before she said, 'I don't think so. I thought I saw . . . well, we can talk when I come up.'

Peggy hung up and waited, glancing every few seconds at the door. Something about the tone of Allison's voice had brought back her former uneasiness. Allison had sounded frightened. Had Mrs. Marvel somehow learned Allison was planning to leave? It would have been just like Allison to tell her so herself, to taunt her with the news.

She glanced at her watch. How long had it been since Allison had called — two minutes, three? Surely she had time to reach the room by now.

The longer Peggy waited, the more uneasy she grew, her glance going again and again to the door, but no knock came. When she looked at her watch again, she saw that another five minutes had gone by.

'She couldn't have forgotten the room number, because she just called me,' she told herself. What else could have happened? Unless an elevator was stuck, there was no reason why it should take close to ten minutes to come from the lobby up to a room.

When another two minutes had gone by, she grabbed her purse from atop the dresser and hurried down to the lobby.

Allison was nowhere to be seen, not in the lobby, not in the restaurant's coffee shop. She saw the house phone on a wall, from which Allison must have called her, but no Allison.

Mrs. Roberts was at the front desk, but she was not very helpful. 'Yes, I think I remember someone like that,' she said. 'Strikingly pretty.'

'Did you see what happened to her?'

Mrs. Roberts pushed back the glasses that had slipped down her nose and screwed up her face thoughtfully.

'No, I can't rightly say I did. I have a vague idea that she left with some people. With a man. No, it was two people, I think, a man and a woman, but I can't be certain.'

Mrs. Roberts shook her head apologetically. 'Really, I'm afraid I'm not being very helpful, but I just didn't notice. I'm not even sure we're talking about the same young woman. You know how it is, so many people come in and out of here every day . . . ' She sighed and shrugged.

'Well, thanks anyway,' Peggy said bleakly. She went out to the sidewalk, looking up and down it as if she expected to see Allison waiting for her there.

Could it have been Waldo and Mrs. Marvel the hotelkeeper saw with Allison? If it was Allison. If they had learned, or intuited, her plans, they might have followed her here and persuaded her somehow to come with them.

Would Allison simply have gone with them without calling Peggy back to explain? It was hard to say. In the last few days Peggy had discovered she hardly knew Allison at all. A week before she would have been certain Allison could not get herself mixed up in a drama as devilish as this.

What should she do now? She hesitated for a moment more. Then, thinking that doing anything was preferable to waiting indecisively, she began to hurry toward the boat landing. If Allison was not at the hotel, the only logical explanation was that for whatever reason she had gone back to Lions Island.

'And if the mountain won't come to Mohammed,' she thought drily, 'Mohammed must go to the mountain.'

⋆ ⋆ ⋆

Once again she found herself approaching the island at night, alone. This time she did not attempt to steal into the place. For one thing, she had no reason to think she would not be allowed to enter freely. Allison had disappeared, true; but Allison had disappeared before, without a word of explanation.

She tied up the boat, rented again from Old George, and started toward the house, but this time the lions' gate was closed and locked.

She rang the bell. It seemed an interminable time, and she was about to ring it again, when she saw Mrs. Brunner trudging along the driveway.

'I'm sorry, Miss, I have instructions that no visitors are permitted,' she said, stopping on the other side of the wrought-iron gate.

'I see,' Peggy said. 'I wonder, is my . . . is Melissa here?'

'She left some time ago.'

'Do you know where she went?'

'I couldn't say, I'm sure.' Mrs. Brunner looked hostile and impatient to get away. She had almost turned to go when Peggy asked, 'Is Mr. Alex here, then? I'd like to see him, if I may.'

'He's not here either. He went to Cleveland, to see the lawyers.' She paused and added, 'He said he wouldn't be back until tomorrow.'

Mrs. Brunner did not wait for any further questions, but strode up the driveway toward the house. In a moment she was out of sight around the curve, not even acknowledging Peggy's feeble 'Thank you.'

Tomorrow. Alex was gone until tomorrow. And if Allison were in some further trouble, tomorrow might be too late.

Peggy walked thoughtfully back to the boat. Suppose — just suppose — that Allison was in further trouble. Suppose, by some means, for some reason, Mrs. Marvel had made her come back to the house. Maybe to iron out their future plans? Or suppose she wouldn't let Allison leave at all.

And if Allison was brought back here against her will, was somehow being kept a prisoner, she was in deadly danger.

She cast off the lines and jumped into the boat, starting up the engine. She steered away from the landing, wondering if anyone on the island were watching her departure. Probably they were, she thought.

When she was far enough away that she knew she would not be seen in the darkness, she switched off the running lights and turned around, heading back to the island, to the place she had tied up before on her first clandestine visit.

⋆ ⋆ ⋆

It was easier this second time, finding her way in, tying the boat to the rocks, wading through the surf. She was wearing a skirt, but it was simple enough to tie it up under her belt until she was on the rocky beach. She stood for a moment, getting her bearings. Then, as before, she began to follow the stone wall, looking for the forgotten door to the inside.

It was still unlocked. She slipped inside, pausing again to listen. There were no signs or sounds of activity down this way. She moved stealthily along the path. This time at least she knew her way about the grounds, was familiar with the house, knew where the back door was. It would be fairly simple to get inside, provided no one saw her.

No one did between the gate and the house. At last she crept across the back lawn, and there were the steps leading up to the kitchen door. There were lights at the kitchen window and she stood in the shadows of a tree for a few minutes, watching. She saw no one moving about inside.

She decided not to chance the kitchen after all. She went instead to the side terrace. The parlor was dark and the French doors unlocked. She hesitated briefly, then pushed the door open and stepped inside.

The thick shadows and the eerie silence gave her a sense of danger. The quiet around her seemed too intense, as if the house were holding its breath. The House of Lions felt alive, and threatening.

She crossed to the fireplace and paused again, listening. The silence seemed to smother her. The scent of a recent fire came from the hearth, and she caught a trace of someone's sweet perfume — Allison's?

She could not remain where she was, listing and waiting for dreaded footsteps in the hall. Her courage seemed to have failed her. She realized that if anything went wrong, if she were attacked or found here, there was no one to hear her scream, no one to come to her rescue.

She slipped into the hall. There were no lights on here either, but the lights from the kitchen and one from upstairs cast a faint glow. She crept on cat's feet toward the kitchen.

There was no one in the kitchen, but across the room the door to the basement stood open. Were they down there? She was about to step into the kitchen when she heard a sound behind her and whirled about. Someone was descending the main stairs. There was no escape by that route. She darted into the kitchen and pressed herself into the niche between the refrigerator and the wall next to it.

She had a glimpse of Mrs. Brunner. The housekeeper went to the cellar stairs and called down, 'There's a boat coming.'

Waldo and Mrs. Marvel appeared at the top of the cellar stairs. Fortunately none of them looked in her direction. They were all in a hurry to get upstairs where they would have a view of the lake.

Peggy waited until they disappeared down the hall. Then, holding her breath, she dashed for the basement door and down the steps.

It was musty and dim down here and a spider's web brushed her arm, almost making her cry out. She paused at the bottom, trying to accustom her eyes to the gloom.

She was in the family's private wine cellar. The racks stretched back into the shadows, filled with bottles of wine: no doubt their best vintages, and great wines from around the world as well.

There was not a sound. Apparently the cellar was empty. Was she on a wild goose chase? What if Allison were not here at all? What if this very moment Allison were waiting at the hotel, wondering what had happened to her?

She was almost convinced to leave, to hurry back to the boat and to town, to see if Allison were really there.

Until she saw the bricks. Piles of them, and a barrow full of mortar as well. And beyond them, a half-finished wall.

Waldo and Mrs. Marvel had been walling off one end of the cellar. Surely an odd occupation for that crew, in the middle of the night . . . unless . . .

She couldn't even bring herself to think of that possibility. She moved with leaden limbs down the remaining few steps, across the narrow width of the wine cellar, to the wall of new bricks. It was almost waist-high, half-finished — a pretty night's work.

She leaned in to look over the wall, and sucked in her breath.

Allison was there, lying in a crumpled heap against the far wall. She didn't need to crawl over the wall, didn't need to touch her cold skin, or see the dried blood that all but obliterated her once-pretty face, to know that Allison was dead.

She did all those things anyway.

Yes, she was dead, her skin already cold to the touch. For a long, agonizing moment Peggy knelt, staring down at the lifeless form that had once been Allison. This was the reward for all her schemes, the result of her reckless machinations. There would be no fortune, no life of ease. She had gambled big, and lost.

But she would not die unavenged, Peggy vowed. She would find the authorities. She would tell them of this grisly wall and its secret. Those who had done this to Allison would pay.

'I swear it, darling,' she whispered. 'I swear, they won't get away with this.'

She wanted to take off her sweater and put it over Allison's face, but she dared not, lest she alert them to the fact that someone had been here and discovered their secret. The last thing she wanted was to alarm them into flight before she brought the authorities back.

The Sheriff would have to listen to her now. This time she wasn't talking about a missing person, she was talking about cold-blooded, brutal murder.

She clambered back over the wall — and stopped dead, as she found herself face to face with Mrs. Marvel.

19

'You,' Mrs. Marvel said, her voice like the hiss of a cobra. 'I might have known — this is all your fault.'

'You killed her,' Peggy said. It was pointless to pretend. The woman had seen her climbing over the half-finished wall.

'She was going to leave, to run out on me. Me, the one who thought all this up, who had made it all work. And she was going to take everything and have me thrown out. She laughed when she told me.'

Peggy's mind darted frantically about, looking for some means of escape, while another part of her kept Mrs. Marvel occupied in talk.

'How did you get her to come back here? She was already at my hotel, on her way up.'

Mrs. Marvel's laugh was a hoarse cackle that echoed through the dusty, cobwebbed cellar. 'That was easy. I appealed to her greed. I told her we had found a new will, changing everything. She was so frightened that she might lose the money after all that she came straight back with us without a moment's hesitation.'

'But why did you kill her?'

Mrs. Marvel came a step closer. The stairs behind her were empty. If only, Peggy thought, I might get to the stairs, up them . . . I'd have a chance to elude them in the dark and reach the boat.

'Because she wouldn't listen to reason,' Mrs. Marvel said, an edge of hysteria creeping into her voice. 'She refused to cooperate, and tried to push past me. She was going to leave again. I picked up a vase and struck her, and when she started to scream, I struck her again, and again.'

Peggy tried to dash past her. She managed to reach the bottom step, but Mrs. Marvel grabbed her arm with such force that she nearly knocked Peggy off her feet. Peggy tried to fight free of those amazingly strong hands, hands that tried to encircle her throat. Peggy slapped at them and reached up, burying her fingers in that elegant gray hair.

To her astonishment the hair came away in her hands, and the veiled hat with it, and Peggy was looking into the evil face of Jack Lions.

He gave a shriek as the hair came loose. 'Waldo!' he screamed. 'Quick!'

He grabbed for his wig as if maintaining his appearance were the most important thing in the world — and in that instant Peggy broke free of him. She stumbled backward into a wine rack, and her clawing fingers closed over a bottle. Jack, his wig askew, lumbered after her. Peggy swung the bottle, catching him alongside the head, and he staggered away from her.

There was only one bare lightbulb overhead. Peggy swung the wine bottle at it. The glass broke and the room was plunged into darkness. Whirling, Peggy ran along the racks of wine.

'What's wrong?' Waldo called from the top of the stairs.

'That bitch, her sister, she's down here and she's found the body. Come on, we've got to find her.'

'What happened to the light?'

'Oh, never mind that, she can't get out of here. Come on!'

Peggy crouched breathlessly behind a row of bottles. Jack, Mrs. Denver, Mrs. Marvel, all one and the same. Their rooms, side by side. Mrs. Marvel's omnipresent veiled hat, Jack's sunglasses. The woman-ish quality she'd sensed in him, and at the same time, the masculine mannerisms of Mrs. Marvel.

If only she'd been clever enough to see. She'd been thrown off by his obvious — or staged — desire for her. Her foolish Leo vanity, he would probably say.

Waldo's heavy footsteps descended the stairs. The two had a whispered consultation. Any second now they would begin to search for her, and somehow she must escape — but how? Jack had said she couldn't get out of here. Were there no windows, no other doors?

She crept along an aisle in a crouched position. Their voices had stopped. She bumped against a bottle, setting it rattling noisily. She darted away, around another corner. Where were they? For all she knew, she might be creeping toward them. There had to be a way out of this basement.

She found one window at last, but it was tiny and high up in the wall. Even if she could get to it, she doubted she would be able to squeeze through it. And they would certainly hear her trying and get to her before she could escape.

She had circled around almost to the stairs again. She listened, and still heard nothing from the two men. She flattened herself against a rack and peered cautiously around it.

The stairs lay open before her. If only she could reach them, get up them, she would be all right. She reached down and slipped her shoes off. Her hands trembled and her legs felt as if they would melt beneath her. She wondered that they did not hear the pounding of her heart.

This is it, she thought; and, taking a deep breath, she dashed from her hiding place toward the stairs. She reached them, grabbing the railing and fairly flinging herself upward. She had forgotten, however, that the two men were not alone in the house. Mrs. Brunner stood at the top of the stairs.

'Stop her,' Mrs. Marvel — Jack — cried from below.

Peggy hesitated, wondering if she could get past the housekeeper, but it was too late, Waldo grabbed her in his powerful arms and dragged her, kicking and struggling, back down to the foot of the stairs, where the fake Mrs. Marvel waited.

'And now,' Jack said, his voice dark with menace, 'we shall have to deal with you, my lovely.'

20

'What'll we do with her?' Waldo asked.

'Do?' Jack chuckled. 'Why, there's only one thing to do. She came back because she wanted to be with her sister, didn't she?'

Peggy felt a chill of horror sweep over her. All the old stories — Edgar Allan Poe's tales — to be buried alive in this musty cellar . . .

'You can't,' she cried, trying again to struggle free, but she was no match for Waldo's brute strength.

'But it's what you wanted, isn't it?' Jack said, laughing. 'I said, that one won't be satisfied until she gets the same as her sister, but he wouldn't listen. Oh, no, she's too pretty, he said, we can't harm her. The ninny, if he'd listened to me we'd have gotten rid of you long ago, that was what I wanted. And I very nearly succeeded, too, the night I sent Waldo to your hotel room. I thought then we'd be

275

finished with you.'

'You . . . you're mad,' Peggy gasped.

'Don't say that,' he shrieked. He waved his hand at the brickwork behind him. 'Put her in there. Tie her up, or better yet, knock her out. By the time she wakes up, she'll be sealed away in her tomb, with her fool of a sister. And we'll be rid of both of them forever.'

Peggy screamed, her cry echoing wildly about the room, but she knew there was no one to hear. Waldo clamped a hand over her mouth and half dragged her, half carried her to the brick wall. She felt herself being lifted bodily over and into the recess next to poor Allison. The room seemed to spin as consciousness threatened to leave her. She fought to retain her senses. The horror of waking up to find herself buried alive was almost more than she could bear.

Her struggles were useless. Waldo tied her hands together and threw her violently into a corner, knocking the breath from her. She lay in a daze and, in the dim light, she saw him spread mortar on a brick, and place another brick atop it.

Then another, and another. It was happening, they were actually sealing her in here with Allison's body.

She screamed again, hysterically, and staggered to her feet, to the brick wall, and tried to push the bricks away, but Waldo gave her another brutal shove, slamming her back against the far wall.

She thought she would go mad . . . thought she *had* gone mad, because even as she stared at the bricks going into place, she saw the wall behind Waldo suddenly swing open — and there, to her amazement, was Alex, with a gun in his hand.

Waldo saw him too and tried to hit him with the brick in his hand, but Alex ducked the blow and instead brought the butt of his gun across the back of Waldo's head. The huge man sagged and fell to the floor in a heap.

Mrs. Brunner gave a cry and rushed to her husband. Jack, wild-eyed, tried to run up the steps, but Alex caught him by a trailing piece of chiffon and jerked him back, nearly off his feet.

'Not so fast,' he said, shoving him back against a wall. 'When I get Peggy out of there, I may send you in to take her place.'

Jack fought, kicking and clawing like a woman, but he was not fighting Peggy now, he was fighting a man who was used to hard work, who had built his muscles working in vineyards and wineries. Jack quickly saw that his struggle was futile, and he collapsed into a wailing, trembling travesty of a heartbroken woman.

'It's all gone wrong,' he sobbed. 'The stars said I couldn't fail, and they lied to me. They lied.'

'Maybe you just read them wrong,' Alex said, stepping across the wall to lift Peggy out. 'Mine said I was going to find the love of my life.'

* * *

Morning light glinted on the water. They stood at the dock watching the launch in which the lake patrol was taking away the prisoners. Jack still wore the lavender chiffon dress he had worn the night before, but in the confusion he had lost his wig and hat. With his makeup smeared, earrings dangling, and his short masculine hair uncovered by any wig, he made a grotesque appearance. He had lost all his spirit, too, and sat staring morosely into the distance.

'You never did say how you happened to come back a day early,' Peggy said, leaning happily into Alex's embrace.

'Partly an odd hunch, call it ESP. Something seemed to be drawing me back. And on top of that, I had forgotten some papers of Father's I needed for the attorneys. I came back for them, and I had gone up to his room when I heard you scream, and the shortest way down to the basement was that secret passageway.'

'How do you suppose Allison knew about that?'

'We'll never know. Maybe Father told her about it himself.'

'Or maybe she really did remember it from her childhood.'

'Maybe. I know one thing. She really wanted to be Melissa, and Father wanted the same thing. And as far as the official reports will show, she was.'

'She'd like that. And I will too.' She

looked across the lake. The launch was nearly out of sight. 'Poor Jack.'

'A real split personality. I think in his mind he really was two different people. Maybe at first it was a deliberate disguise. He was here in the house, but he was insignificant. Nobody paid any attention to him. But he knew Father was into astrology, and he knew the old man pined for his lost Melissa. Somehow, Jack introduced Mrs. Marvel into the house and into Father's confidence. And I think over the years he really came to think of her as another person entirely. Probably he really did hate her, because she had come to dominate him, she was so much stronger than he was.'

'But he still had the other side to his personality. I think when he was Jack, he really was attracted to me.'

'Leo vanity, that's all,' he said teasingly, giving her waist a squeeze.

'Oh, no.' She pulled away from him and stared, shaking her head.

'What's wrong?' he asked, puzzled.

'That's how all this started — with astrology, and Leo, and lions.'

He laughed and pulled her back into his embrace. 'And that's how it will end, too. After all, you're going to be a Lion. Mrs. Alex Lions.'

They were near the gate. When at last their kiss ended, she looked up, past his shoulder, at one of the great stone beasts overhead. In the past, the lions had frightened her, but now this one looked benign and protective — like the Leo of her sign.

THE END

We do hope that you have enjoyed reading this large print book.

Did you know that all of our titles are available for purchase?

We publish a wide range of high quality large print books including:
Romances, Mysteries, Classics
General Fiction
Non Fiction and Westerns

Special interest titles available in large print are:
The Little Oxford Dictionary
Music Book, Song Book
Hymn Book, Service Book

Also available from us courtesy of Oxford University Press:
Young Readers' Dictionary
(large print edition)
Young Readers' Thesaurus
(large print edition)

For further information or a free brochure, please contact us at:
Ulverscroft Large Print Books Ltd.,
The Green, Bradgate Road, Anstey,
Leicester, LE7 7FU, England.
Tel: (00 44) **0116 236 4325**
Fax: (00 44) **0116 234 0205**